Blood Brothers

Faerie King, Volume 1

Ashlyn Pierce

Published by Ashlyn Pierce, 2021.

Table of Contents

To my parents, with love.

CHAPTER ONE

I'm running through a field of red flowers. My heart is thrashing in my chest, desperate to get away from the monster behind me.

I can't breathe.

Too bright, the sun blinds me. I begin to panic. How am I going to get away from the beast chasing me if I can't *see*?

I have to keep going. I can't stop. My eyes are glued to the ground, the only thing I can see in this white light.

The flowers, covered in the blood of the monster's victims, fade away behind me.

The ground inclines sharply, some patch of grass grips hold of my toes. My knees hit the ground.

No.

I can hear the monster panting behind me, much closer now.

My feet slip on the wet grass, and it takes a lifetime to get them under me. He's coming.

I know I'm going to die now. I took too long.

And now I can feel his breath on my neck.

A cool breeze caresses my shoulders. It forces the clouds to conceal the sun, and through the haze I can see a mansion up ahead.

I feel the *thing* behind me getting closer, trying to bring me down. I force my legs to propel my body forward. I'm tired, and I'm slowing down against my will.

His breathing is so close now.

The house begins to slip away, out of my reach.

"No!" I scream.

I try to run faster. But my legs feel like lead; and my body is suddenly heavy. It's like trying to run underwater and I can't do it. This is the end.....

I gasped and jerked off the ground. It took a second for my eyes to adjust to the afternoon light; I looked around frantically. Somewhere close, a waterfall gurgled softly. It was just a dream; I scrambled to my feet.

Just a dream. I took a deep breath.

But it had seemed so real...Another soft breeze wafted across my face, blowing tendrils of hair in my face. I shoved them back, the image of the bloody flowers still sharp behind my eyes. I half-expected to see them when I turned to glance behind me.

The golden light of sunset blazed in the meadow around me, setting everything alight. Dense forest encroached on the meadow, shadowy and sinister. I trembled, feeling so exposed as I stood alone in the halo of light that encircled me. It reminded me of the nightmare.

I fought off another shudder and hastened toward the protection of the forest.

The path I walked along was well-worn, I had to be careful. I listened intently as I moved. I could have sworn someone was behind me. Someone was watching. I couldn't help looking over my shoulder, hoping to catch a glimpse of whoever or whatever it was.

Nothing was there. And the uneasy feeling in my chest remained.

Thunder rumbled above my head. Great. I picked up the pace, forgetting the unseen presence in my hurry.

It was pouring by the time I sloshed up the driveway. The sight of the house—all the lights on, smoke swirling from the chimney—filled me with relief. Mom was home, and the house would be warm.

The warm scent of molasses cookies swept over me as I came in. My hands pulled my hood down and unzipped my jacket as I kicked off rain-soaked shoes on the way to the kitchen.

The room was dim; I could see that one lightbulb was not working. I sighed, and turned my eyes to the little stove in the corner.

My mother was pulling out a batch, trying to get it safely to the counter one-handed as she pushed her thick black hair out of her eyes. She gave me a rebuking look.

"Bethany, where've you been? You've been gone for hours."

Uh oh. I stole a cookie off the counter. "Cookies are good, Mom."

But Mom tossed her oven mitt to the counter and faced me, hands on her hips. There was no way I was going to get away with my secret. I scowled.

"I was going for a walk. Down past the dirt road." I bit into the cookie and took off my jacket, placing it on the back of one of the cherrywood chairs. It felt impossible to look her in the eye.

"Baby, you know I don't like you going down that way with Jerry Thomson living across the street."

"It's not a street, Mom. It barely even qualifies as a trail."

She shot me a dirty look and turned to her baking. "Don't you have homework to do?"

"No." But since we both knew that I did, I spun around and headed up the stairs, bringing my backpack along with me. I threw it on the bed and locked the door behind me before I changed into some dry clothes, and got out my books. As I worked, the light outside the window darkened. I looked up, puzzled.

The atmosphere in my room had changed. It was murky, dusty, and hard to breathe. I frowned. Strange; the air didn't smell of smoke, but maybe Mom had burned something.

I hopped off the bed and yanked the door open. "Mom?"

No answer.

I went over to the railing to peer downstairs. The air was worse down there, almost red in color. What was going on?

"Mom," I called, this time not expecting an answer. Something was wrong. I set off down the stairs, worrying about freakish gas leaks or biological attacks.

The living room was empty, and, when I got there, so was the kitchen. My hand rose to my throat automatically as I breathed in the thick, sour air. My lungs burned with the scent of it. I felt like the fog was pressing in on me, trying to push me to the floor and crush me.

Thunder roared in the distance; the windows were bathed in rain. A reddish tint reflected off the wetness. The pine tree in our front yard snapped back and forth violently.

My hands grasped the window and pulled it open, desperate for fresh air. I threw my head out and gasped.

No stars, just a small clear area in the sky where I could see a part of the moon: bright red, as though someone had smeared it with blood.

"Don't ever go out when the full moon is red, Bethany," I remembered my mother telling me once. "It can only bring evil to you." I shivered, and shut the window, remembering.

"Why, Momma?"

Mom's voice was so soft I could hardly hear her. "There's an old family legend...the moon burns red when someone declared war against the fairies. Or when the fairies declare war on her. It's a warning."

"So how does the moon find out?" My brow furrowed. It was only a scary story, of course, but I didn't like not understanding.

"It doesn't. The king of the fairies has a special friend. He's in charge of how the moon looks on our side. Like a mask. He knows when to warn and when to comfort." Mom had laughed then, at the look on my serious little face.

"Just a story, sweetie," she said, the faux gravity gone from her voice.

Footsteps sounded on the cellar steps, startling me out of my daydream. The air was clear again, but I hardly noticed. The footsteps had disturbed me.

My hands reached for the counter, blindly searching for a weapon as my eyes glued themselves to the door. Suddenly, I did not want to be alone here.

My mother's dark head poked through the doorway, and I felt my body relax.

"Dinner's going to be late," she mumbled, oblivious to my terror. "I thought we had some vegetables downstairs for soup but apparently not. I'm going to have to think of something else."

"Oh," the breath blew out of me. "That's okay, Mom. I'm not really hungry anyway." My hands were still shaking; I hid them in my pockets.

The next morning, I rushed to get to school through the deluge of rain that had continued to fall. As I pulled into the parking lot, I saw Marissa waiting outside for me.

I chuckled. We'd known each other since we were six, and I couldn't remember a time when she'd ever gone to school by herself. I got out of the car and slammed the door shut. One would think that with her new boyfriend and all, she wouldn't feel the need to wait for me.

One would think.

"Hurry up!" she called to me through the downpour. I jogged up the steps and we went in together. Marissa took her jacket off as soon as she was inside; she ran her hand through her short frizzy hair. I left my jacket on, cold as usual.

I spotted Jason coming down the hallway before she did; but then she *did* see him. She kissed me on the cheek with a chipper "See ya" and skipped off.

I put my hands in my pockets, watching them go with apprehension.

Marissa clamped onto his arm and started talking a mile a minute. Jason's stiff expression didn't change as he spoke to her; he rolled his eyes over her head, towards me.

He winked. I curled my hands into fists.

Feeling his eyes on my back the whole time, I turned a full three-sixty and marched to Government without looking back. It hadn't started yet, and I was able to get a good seat. I felt bad for whoever had to take the chairs up front. Mr. Reese had a way of teaching and giving a swimming class at the same time. I gagged a little as I thought of it. How could he still be teaching? It was unsanitary.

I knew the lesson backwards and forwards, so it did nothing to hold my attention. I spent the next fifty minutes doodling aimlessly in my notebook. It wasn't till the bell rang and class ended that I realized I'd been drawing the face of the monster in my nightmare. Aggravated, I tore the page out.

Spanish was a little better since I had to really concentrate to understand it. Samantha Berkley whispered translations in my ear during class, and—when Miss Rodriguez wasn't looking—I slipped her a five. By then it was time for lunch, I put my books in my bag and took off towards the cafeteria, where I knew Marissa would be waiting.

She was sitting near the windows, picking at a salad.

"Hey, where's Jason?" I asked as I came up to her. I hoped he wouldn't be eating with us today. She looked up, taken aback by my tone.

"Probably still in class. Why, what's up?"

"Nothing."

She took a bite of her salad, eyeing me shrewdly. "Are you okay?"

I slipped into the chair beside her. "I'm fine," I said, though I instantly knew by the look on her face that she wasn't buying it. Marissa knew me too well.

"You look pale."

I laughed. "I didn't sleep well last night, I guess."

"Mmmm. I understand." She nodded, thinking about the thunderstorm, probably. I relaxed a little bit and gulped some soda. There was no reason to tell her I'd been having nightmares every night; she'd probably just tell Jason anyway.

"What are you doing after school?" she asked, looking down.

"I don't know yet." I glimpsed around the lunchroom as I spoke. Even though the lights were bright, the opaque darkness of the sky outside the cafeteria window and the deep blue chairs and tiles on the checkered floor made it seem darker in here than it really was. Kids were everywhere, talking and laughing, I even spotted a few people that looked like they were crying. The noise was horrendous, but I enjoyed it. It made me feel safer, though I didn't know why it made me feel that way.

The thunder rolled, I could feel the vibrations on the table, under my hands.

Marissa leaned away. "Whoa....That's weird."

I could hear exclamations from a few other students as well. Outside the window, the trees were whipping around sharply. A trash can rolled across the parking lot.

I hoped it didn't hit somebody's car on the way through.

And then Principle Stone was there. I snapped out of my reverie and turned to pay attention. No one seemed to see him there. I tapped Marissa's arm, and she frowned at him.

"What is he doing here?"

I just shook my head, keeping my eyes on him. The dread I'd felt this morning washed through me. I wasn't sure I wanted to know. Principle Stone wiped his face with a kerchief and glanced around the room. From where I sat it seemed as though he were squinting. I noticed his hands were tightly clenched.

"Hey!"

No one heard. The noise in the room continued.

"Hey. Everybody listen up!" A different voice yelled.

The room silenced. Everybody watched him with wary expressions, especially me.

Principle Stone looked around the room warily. "Thank you....I've just been notified that we're in for a nasty storm in about an hour or so. It's coming in from Portland, and they've already got some trees and power lines down there. I really don't want any of you kids getting stuck out here, I know quite a few of you come in from quite a ways......"

He paused then, and my breath caught. What was happening? "So school's out for the rest of today. The pep rally is not going to happen. We're going to have to reschedule....." he paused, clasping his hands together, "thanks for listening, and I suggest that you all get started for home as soon as you can, okay? Okay. See you guys tomorrow."

Marissa popped out of her chair and threw her jacket over her shoulders. She grabbed me under the elbow and tugged. "C'mon," she murmured.

I leaned over to get my bag, then walked with Marissa to the door. It was cram-full of students trying to make an escape, their expressions ranging from excitement to apprehension. We had to wait for a long time before we could finally shove our way through.

"Let's go find Jason."

I shook my head. "He'll be fine, Marissa, trust me. We'll never find him in this crowd.

"Come on, let's go."

She went with me, but it irritated me that she kept looking back. I wanted to tell her to let it go, it's just a thunderstorm, but I couldn't when I was just as nervous as she was. Maybe even more. We got out the door—and stopped, stunned by the sudden burst of wind and rain in our faces. Marissa edged a little closer to me.

"I don't want to drive all the way back through this!" she yelled. I could hardly hear her with the wind in my ears.

"Follow me back to my place!" I hollered back. She nodded.

We ran arm in arm across the lot, trying to keep each other from being blown away by the gale. Marissa reached her car first and leaped inside while I made a mad dash for mine. Without my best friend to hold me down, the wind shoved me around. I nearly ran up against the hood of a car, but I grabbed hold of the truck beside it and walked myself back.

I reached my car, unlocked the door as quickly as my shaking wet hands could manage, and threw myself inside. I could see the taillights of Marissa's Jeep as she backed out and stopped, waiting for me to take the lead. Gingerly, I put my car in reverse.

A horn shrieked. I slammed my foot on the brakes. My body flew up against the back of the seat.

The black pickup roared past me. I rolled my eyes and started out again. This time, I made it to where Marissa sat, waiting. I led her out of the throng of cars, hoping it would get easier once we hit the road home.

It didn't.

The wind was horrible. It took everything I had just to keep the car straight. And the rain only made it less manageable. I clung to the wheel and drove slowly, checking my mirrors every millisecond to see if Marissa was still there.

Once I thought I saw a man standing at the side of the road. He stood there in the shadows, watching traffic go by with a set expression on his hollow face. But when I looked again, all I could see through the rain was blackness.

I frowned.

Lightning crashed overhead, blinding me with a blast of white light. The road vanished from sight. I rammed my foot against the brake in panic. The car shuddered for a second, then veered to the left, carrying me off the road, then stopping.

I sat there for a moment, dazed. It was black again, and I could see nothing without my headlights on. I turned them back on and backed onto the road once more. Marissa followed behind me still, and I didn't go off the road again.

A little ways down the road, the wind grew worse, I had to slow down further and grip the wheel with both hands to keep my car in the right lane. A couple of crazies passed us on the way through, blowing through traffic at sixty miles an hour through the flooded streets.

Once, I saw a tree branch snap off and tumble in front of one of them. My heart panged wildly and I hit the brakes again, giving the driver space to move back in the line. He did. He stayed there for the rest of the way back.

It took us thirty minutes to reach the house, where it normally took me only ten. We dove out into the rain, pulling our hoods close around our faces and racing for the door. Marissa found the key and let us in. We were both panting by the time we got inside and had ripped off our hoods.

"Woo!" she exclaimed as I removed my shoes. "Wow. That was bad."

I laughed breathlessly in agreement. Marissa took off her shoes and jacket, knowing where to put them, then followed me to the kitchen.

"I'm going to call Mom really quick. I want to make sure she's okay."

"'Kay." Marissa responded wearily; she clopped off to raid the refrigerator.

Mom didn't answer her office phone, so I tried her cell. It rang twice and then I heard a click on the other end.

"Hello?"

"Mom! Where are you?"

"I'm headed to a meeting right now." Mom sounded surprised. "Are you okay, honey? Why aren't you in school?"

"Principle Stone kicked us out. We're having a really bad storm over here, I just wanted to call and see if you were okay."

"Oh," she laughed, relieved. "I am."

"Bethany! Where do you keep the chocolate?"

"Is that Marissa?"

"Yeah, Mom. She didn't want to drive all the way home. Can't blame her, really. We almost gone blown clear off the road heading back." I *did* get blown off, but I wasn't going to tell my mother that. I wondered why Marissa hadn't mentioned it when we got in. Hadn't she seen me go into the ditch? Vaguely, I heard my mom's voice.

"It's that bad?"

"Uh-huh."

"B!"

"I have to let you go—see you tonight, Mom. I love you."

"I love you too, honey. Stay in the house."

Why would I go outside? I hung up the phone and turned to face Marissa. She was perched upon the counter, rifling through the cupboards madly.

"We don't have chocolate, Marissa."

Marissa froze. She stared at me, shocked. "No?" she whimpered.

"Nope. Do you want to call Jason? I'm sure he's back by now."

"Yeah." She hopped down and walked past me. She gave me a nasty look. "I can't believe you don't have any candy here."

I shrugged and shot a look out the window. The rain hadn't let up. I waited patiently while Marissa talked to Jason. Her obsession with him was getting a little old, but I was hoping she'd grow out of it pretty soon. Otherwise I'd have to take matters into my own hands. I turned away from the window as she hung up.

"So what do we do now?" she asked, putting her hands on her hips and frowning out at the rain.

"Hmm..."

"Bethany?"

Her tone caught me off guard; I turned to her. "What?"

She wasn't looking at me, doodling imaginary figure-eights on the countertop with her finger. "I wanted to talk to you. About something—" She didn't finish. I took a deep breath and held it, rolling my eyes before I spoke.

"Jason." I frowned. In the periphery, I thought I saw her nod once. "What about him?" I had to ask, even though I was pretty certain I already knew.

"He's been acting weird lately and I don't know why. He wants to see you more and more and even when we're alone, he acts distracted."

She looked at me then, and I met her eyes evenly. I didn't like the picture she was painting.

"I've already told you what I think."

"I know." She started fidgeting again and I resisted the urge to scowl. "I guess I just wondered if you'd changed your mind is all."

"No."

"I—"

"Why don't you go talk to him about this if you're so concerned? It has nothing to do with me."

CHAPTER TWO

Later, after we'd both gone to bed, I lay back under the warm covers, scowling at the ceiling. It wasn't fair. After all I'd done for her, all the years we'd known each other, my best friend still didn't trust me not to steal her boyfriend. As if I wanted him.

I'd known Jason years before she'd even met him, and even as kids I'd thought he was creepy. There was something about his personality—too clingy, too much darkness broiling beneath the charming exterior—that made me mistrust him.

I'd told her so the minute I found out they were dating.

How dare she assume such a thing? Of course I knew where it came from: Jason's sly winks, his yearning stares from across the cafeteria. I'd noticed them all and so, apparently, had Marissa, which surprised me. Up till now she'd never said a word about it.

I sighed and rolled over, exhausted. Maybe in the morning things would be better. I closed my eyes and succumbed to sleep.

And then awoke.

The storm had ceased, and my room was completely quiet now. Not a sound came from outside. I had no idea what had awakened me. I lay tense, listening to the silence. Had I imagined the presence I felt? Or was it just another dream? I stared at the light that poured onto my bed from the hallway, trying to pinpoint the cause of my unease.

Then it hit me—I hadn't left the door open. I shot a glance at the closed door, then back to the light. The hair on my arms stood upright, and I trembled. Slowly, I rolled my body towards the window.

A shriek pierced my ears. I slapped my hand over my mouth and sat up, clutching the blankets close to my pounding heart.

The sky was a deep, glowing crimson. Dark clouds streaked across the midnight sky from behind a bright moon, casting eerie shadows on the lawn and menace to the pitch black forest.

But, though frightening, this was not what had forced the scream out of me. For, in the light of the moon I had spotted a face—a horrible contorted face—staring at me through the curtains.

And then it was gone, disappeared into the darkness. I sat there for a long time staring at the spot where the face had been; unable to move.

When I could move again, I jumped out of bed. I couldn't stay here after what I'd just seen. I had to get out of this room. Halfway down the steps, I heard the front door click shut. I froze, listening hard. The kitchen light turned on. Slowly, I inched my way down and peeked around the corner.

It was Mom, she was just tossing her keys to the counter. I sighed and went up to her.

"Hey, honey." She hugged me.

"Mom," I greeted her, trying to keep my voice from shaking. "How was your drive home?"

She rolled her eyes. "Horrible, thanks for warning me. Marissa's still here?"

"Yeah."

She nodded and pulled the rubber band out of her hair. I thought about telling her about our fight but decided against it. I was too tired for the amount of talking that entailed.

"Goodness that moon is frightening tonight."

My stomach rolled. I tried not to look at the windows, afraid I'd see the face again. "Sure is."

"I've never seen it quite that color before. It's strange," she mused on.

I only shivered.

Mom laughed as she kicked off her heels. "You know, your grandmother used to tell me stories about that. She used to say it meant trouble for fairy people when the moon got red like that." She laughed quietly again. A wave of relief coursed through my veins; I folded my arms over my chest.

"Fairy people? I thought it meant something bad was going to happen."

"Oh, it means that too." She smiled. "Especially for the friends of fairies. They're the ones that have to leave their world behind."

I could feel my eyes widen and tried to relax. Fairies aren't real. I leaned against the leather sofa and watched her. "What else does it mean?"

"Oh, Bethany. They're only stories."

"I know. But I want to know. It's interesting."

"Well—" Mom thought for a moment. "According to some old Indian stories, if the moon was turned red in your seventeenth year it meant you could never have children. Something about dangerous toxins in the air."

"No?"

Mom smirked. "*No.* I made that up."

"Oh." I tried to look like I'd known that all along, but I wasn't fooling her. She patted me on the back.

"Get some rest, Bethany." She kissed my cheek. "You have school tomorrow."

I climbed the stairs back up to my room and curled up under the covers. The moon was too bright for me to sleep, so I hopped up and slammed the curtains shut. That helped some. When I sank down on the bed again, I fell asleep instantly.

Marissa was up when I came downstairs that morning. She pushed a cup of coffee towards me, across the table. A peace offering. I took it and leaned against the counter tiredly.

"I really don't want to go to school today," she grumbled.

I took a sip of the strong coffee. "Won't see Jason," I replied, smoothing out my hair with my free hand and looking at her out of the corner of my eye. As much as I disliked him, he was good for keeping my best friend in school. Before she'd met him, there'd been a time when I had thought for sure she was going to drop out. I just hoped the reference wouldn't spark another argument.

"Yeah, that's true," she murmured, twirling her earring around with one hand, feeding herself coffee with the other. She looked defeated. I smiled.

I STOOD AT THE END of the line, my hands tightening around the edges of the plastic tray in my hands. Jason had moved in on my seat next to Marissa; I didn't miss that there was an extra seat now, on his other side. I frowned, letting my eyes gaze about the room.

I caught sight of Vicky then, and she waved me over. I shot one more glance at Marissa's table. She was deep in conversation with Jason and didn't notice me.

Jason nodded somewhat absentmindedly to whatever she'd just said and glimpsed over his shoulder at me.

I ignored his look, abruptly turning towards Vicky's table. As I got closer, I noticed her eyes were fire red around the rims. She was wiping her nose with a tissue.

"Whoa..." I murmured, sitting down. "You look sick."

"I know," she said. It sounded like "I doe." I smiled sympathetically.

She nodded towards Jason and Marissa. "How long have dey beed going out?"

"Three weeks."

She read the look on my face with dark, clever eyes. "You don't care for the idea?"

I shook my head. "They're too different."

"Ah." She sneezed, then shrugged. "Well, you never doe, dey might surprise you."

I shrugged.

"Did you have to drive through that storm yesterday?" she asked, changing the subject.

I nodded. "It was awful."

"I guess half of Portland is out of power."

I raised my eyebrows and let them fall quickly; took another bite of my sandwich. Marissa's loud, melodic laugh rang through the cafeteria. I shot a look over my shoulder and shook my head.

Vicky chuckled.

The remainder of the day wore on. I was afraid to be alone. And of going home. No matter how many times I told myself that I was being silly, tried to convince myself that it was all just a nightmare, I couldn't stop waiting, expecting the face to pop up again somewhere, when I was least expecting it.

It hadn't been a nightmare, and I knew it.

When I got home, I decided to take a walk down by the waterfall.

The sun was shining as I walked down the road to the dirt lane, a welcome change from the past couple of days.

Old man Thomas's shack sat on one side of the lane, a dilapidated one room house that looked like it'd been slapped together with old barn wood and rusty nails. The front yard was covered in old rusty cars and beer cans. Grass grew several feet in most places, as his lawnmower had broken down years ago and he'd never bothered to fix it; much less spend the money to get a new one.

I started jogging when I got close to his place and didn't slow till I was concealed among the trees. I cut across the forest then, meandering through the dark shadows of conifers and apple trees.

As I walked, the air became heavy and somber. The forest was still as death. I listened futilely for the sound of the birds singing and shivered. My forest was never like this. I kept going, hoping in the back of my mind that everything would be normal once I reached the waterfall again.

Once I reached the spot, I slowed my pace, walking as quietly as possible. I felt exposed again, marching into the heart of the meadow in this silence. I turned around in a circle, trying to pinpoint the reason for my apprehension.

There was none that I could see. Everything was still. The sun reflected the rain drops from yesterday's storm on spider webs and leaves of grass. They glittered like diamonds in the bright day. The ferns and tall wildflowers swayed in the slight breeze indifferently. The huge green trees that surrounded me revealed nothing, I could hear the rushing of the waterfall behind me, but nothing else.

Nothing out of the ordinary.

I let out a deep, shuddering sigh. Maybe I should go back.....

Something snapped behind me.

I whirled around. The pine branch at the edge of the meadow was swinging back and forth, I heard something scurry away. It sounded huge.

My breath caught; terror nearly drove me insane. I followed the path the sound was taking with my eyes, and for a second I saw a form darting through a small patch of light.

Then there was nothing again.

I didn't move.

It felt like eons later that I dared to take a step. It was slow, however, cautious. I concentrated hard, but the sound never reached my ears again. I made it to the edge of the meadow, and then I started running.

I stumbled as I plowed through the uneven forest. Once, I caught my shoe under a big root and went pitching down the hill.

But I didn't want to stop. I got to my feet again and set off at an even brisker pace than before. I dashed out onto the trail, twisting both my ankles in the effort and bruising my shin. I felt like I was running from the monster in my dreams again.

I didn't slow down until I got back onto the main road. Even then I kept looking over my shoulder, expecting to see something—though

I wasn't sure yet what—following me. I could feel the sinister presence at my back the whole way home. It was still there even after I had shut and locked the door.

Mom stared at me, holding two plates in her hands. "What's wrong, Bethany? Are you okay?"

I must look awful, I thought as I stood, panting in the threshold. I didn't want to tell her about the meadow. She'd never let me go back there again, and I would probably get an "I told you about that man" lecture.

It hadn't been old man Thomas that much I knew.

"Bethany." She was anxious now, staring at me with a distressed expression.

I tried to focus. "I...Saw something....An animal, I think....Out in the woods."

Mom cocked her head to the side, it was obvious she knew I wasn't telling her something, but she didn't push it.

"Are you all right?" she demanded through tight lips.

"Yeah. Fine. Don't worry, Mom, it was probably just a bunny or something."

"Hmmm." She nodded, busying herself with the table. I wondered when she was going to let the hammer fall, and jogged upstairs. Maybe it would blow over while I was out of sight.

Once I was safely in my room, I shut my door behind me and collapsed on the bed. I couldn't do anything but lay there, trying not to think about what'd just happened, wishing I understood what was happening.

An annoying voice in my head told me I probably didn't want to understand.

Mom called me down for dinner. I sat up slowly and rolled over to get out of bed. A movement caught my eye. A form...a face.....I couldn't breathe. Watching me again.

There was a blur of darkness, and a bang. And then it was all gone. The lights flickered for the briefest second, but I hardly noticed. I stared out the window, terrified.

After a long moment, I got up.

I went quickly to the window and peeked out. I saw the quick, lithe form I had encountered in the woods scampering into the forest. Just a little more than a blur. I shut the curtains hastily and turned my back to the window.

"Bethany!"

"Coming, Mom!" I called back and shot another peek out the window. I went downstairs, more disturbed than ever.

I didn't want to go to bed tonight. I wanted to stay up and watch TV and pretend like nothing was wrong.

We ate in silence. Mom kept shooting me looks from across the table, but I ignored her. I dreaded having to go back upstairs again. After supper, I volunteered to do the dishes, an offer that made my mother frown. She didn't object, though, and when I was done with that, I sat down on the couch and watched TV beside her, neither of us speaking.

The moon was red again that night. The light ran straight through my thin curtains and spilled out onto the floor. As much as I tried to ignore it, it still troubled me. Once, I was certain someone had moved in front of my window; the form cast long shadows across my room.

I had jumped and nearly screamed. But when I turned over, it was gone. Only the reddish hue was visible through the curtains. I lay back, wishing I had thicker curtains.

I wondered if I was going insane, or just paranoid. I preferred to believe the latter, but I had to wonder whether I was seeing things. One thing was for sure, I wasn't going back to the waterfall anytime soon.

I'M IN A HUGE MEADOW. It's the most beautiful sight I've ever seen: the very trees are sparkling with surreal colors and very bright. It's hard for my eyes to adjust to the strange light, but it's so peaceful…I realize I'm wearing a flowing white dress that matches the lovely roses that blanket the earth at my feet.

The meadow explodes. Or seems to. I squeeze my eyes shut, expecting to be blown to bits, but nothing happens. Nothing changes.

My meadow has erupted with the violent clash of battle. It's so loud…I cover my ears.

Through the din, I hear someone calling my name. And I don't know why, but I have to go to him.

To find him.

I run towards the sound of his voice, and stop when I get to the top of a large hill.

Before me, thousands of men are engaged in a tremendous fight. Blood is everywhere, spilling out of bodies and staining the gorgeous white roses red.

"Bethany!"

I whirl around but I can't see him. Where *is* he? My heart goes to war against my lungs inside my chest.

He calls me in the distance again…

My shoulders are seized. I am spun around so suddenly and forcefully my head snaps back and I find myself looking into the hideous face from my window. The monster is squeezing my arms too tightly, and now I'm wishing that the man would come find *me*. I can't help myself this time.

I scream.

CHAPTER THREE

Marissa wasn't in school. I knew the instant I pulled into the lot and didn't find her waiting outside the door. It was just as well, I supposed. After my nightmare last night I wasn't particularly looking forward to having company.

I went through the day on autopilot, a hollow shell of myself. I felt like a robot as I went to my classes, took notes, got my food....all without consciously deciding to do so. My mind was in another world entirely.

I only vaguely heard Vicky report that Marissa had caught the flu from Tanya Rivers; which should have surprised me because Marissa never hangs out with Tanya Rivers but somehow it didn't. At the moment, I had little interest in what was going on in Marissa's life.

I saw Tanya in gym a few hours later, red cheeked and bursting with energy. I couldn't help but wonder whether Vicky had been wrong. Or was Marissa just getting back into the habit of missing school? Maybe she'd had a fight with Jason.

I forgot about it as soon as the bell sounded. When it was time to leave, I lingered in the doorway, a sudden burning desire to stay tugged at my chest. But I knew I couldn't do that. I stepped outside and walked over to my car, fidgeting nervously with my purse as I went along.

The cold air swirled around me, it cut through my jacket like a knife. I shivered and wrapped my coat around myself tightly as I reached the car, skimming my surroundings. I was the only one in the lot.

And yet...I could have sworn I felt someone standing behind me. *Stop being crazy.*

I shoved my key into the lock, lifted my eyes to the reflection in the window. My breath stopped.

He was there, reaching for me. His hollow features cold and dead, my body tensed as his fingers grazed against the back of my jacket....

I whirled around to face him. Dark cascades blinded me. I couldn't see! I pawed the hair out of my face, eyes searching for the stranger.

He was gone. I spun in circles, still pushing the hair out of my eyes. Searching. It reminded me of the nightmare the night before. Only this was different, because this time I was looking out of fear.

I put my shaking hand on the door handle, trying to suppress the sudden leaden pounding resonating through my chest. It wasn't a pounding like the heavy beating of my heart when I was frightened. No, this was a feeling that rocked my entire body; a force fighting to escape my chest. I took a deep breath.

The whole way home, I kept thinking about the man that was tagging along behind me, watching. The idea made me sick. I had to stay around people. I had to stay out of the open.

Unfortunately, tonight my socializing had to end at the house. Mom wasn't home yet, and everyone that I knew was probably at Jay's house. Some party or something Marissa had tried to convince me to go to. I didn't even know where that was. I made up for my lack of company by locking all the windows and doors and shutting all the curtains. By the time I was done it was so dark that I had to turn on the house lights. All of them. It felt silly, but it also made me feel a lot more secure.

The phone rang once, sending my heart clear up into my throat. I steadied myself.

"Hello?" My voice was shaking, I tried to clear it.

"Bethany? It's Tracy." I relaxed instantly at the sound of my big sister's familiar voice. "Are you okay?"

"Yeah. Fine. What's up?"

Tracy said she was coming over for a few days. "Don't tell Mom, though," she warned, just before hanging up. I smiled at that. Tracy and her surprises.

The sight of the closed curtains instantly reminded me of my plight, I tried to ignore them as much as possible and get my homework done.

Mom seemed surprised when she came home and found the house on lockdown. She looked at me questioningly, but I didn't offer an explanation. I didn't need her thinking I was crazy, too.

I wasn't crazy. I *had* seen someone out in the woods, and that someone was the same one I'd seen in my window. Though how he'd gotten away so fast, I didn't know; I just knew it was real. I considered telling Mom, but decided not to. The last thing I wanted to do was cause a panic. Or an appointment with a therapist.

That night the moon was back to normal. The sight of that pristine, white orb filled me with ecstasy. My trial was over. Everything was going to get back to normal, now.

The moon doesn't tell the future, stupid my mind told me. Still, I fell asleep easily after that.

I'M RUNNING THROUGH the woods, trying to get to my car before Marissa does. She's running beside me. She looks at me. So scared.

Something is behind us. I turn to look, and my foot catches on something. I fall. I'm stuck.

"Marissa!" I scream, but she just keeps running.

And then the forest is ripped away. The wind and rain batter me violently. I'm trying so hard, but I can't....I can't stand up. The weight of gravity is pushing down on me, crushing my ribs. It's as though the very earth refuses to let me get up.

But I do.

The last thing I see, is the moon.

The blood-dyed moon.

I SCREAMED, CLUTCHING my pillow tight. I cast a glance out the window. The moon shone, clear and bright. I relaxed. It was only a dream. I wondered how long this could go on before I really went insane.

The next day I was the subject of many "you should have been there" stories about Jay's party. I suffered through them all patiently, knowing that by tomorrow they would have all forgotten about it. After school, rather than going home, I went to the library to study.

"Hey."

I looked up. "Hey, Jason."

"Have you seen Marissa and Tanya anywhere?"

I made a face and shook my head, scribbling in my notebook. "Sorry."

A few minutes later, I saw Marissa come in. She looked around wildly, as though confused. I caught her eye and pointed.

"Thank you!" she mouthed and hurried off.

About an hour later they left. Somehow Tanya had been added to the group; as she passed me, she gave me a dirty look that I did not understand.

I logged out of the computer and collected my books. I swung the book bag strap over my shoulder.

And stopped.

There was a man standing at the front desk. His stance, and something about the way he moved struck me as sickeningly familiar. As I watched, he turned.

My heart turned over. His hollow eyes burned holes in my head. I stared back, too terrified to even consider looking away. A throbbing started in my chest and resonated through my body. I inhaled, and my head spun. I realized that I had ceased to breathe the instant I saw him and forced myself to inhale.

The sneer faded from his face. The man glared at me openly, leaning against the desk. The throbbing got worse. I began to tremble. It felt like something was crushing me, the pulsating that had originated in my heart made it hard to breathe. What was wrong with me?

I blinked. He was gone when I opened my eyes again.

Adrenaline bled into my system, making it impossible to sit still. I shot out of my seat and flew towards the doors. Cold air spilled over my shoulders. I ran to my car and threw myself inside.

What was happening?

CHAPTER FOUR

I locked the house down that night just to be safe. But the terrifying unseen presence I'd felt for the past couple of days wasn't there. The moon glowed, crisp and white that night; it was such a wonderful change from the macabre haze that I slept with the curtains wide open, enjoying the light.

I awoke the next morning, refreshed. I rolled over, and sighed, enjoying the peace. I seriously considered staying home when my alarm went off.

But then Marissa would come looking for me.

Something moved out of the corner of my eye. I paused, seeing only the branches of the lilac tree swing back and forth. My emotions whirled around in a baffling maelstrom. I shook my head.

It felt safer on the road and at school, where there were people everywhere. I found I was able to relax slightly.

Marissa still wasn't at school, though, and Tanya wasn't in gym.

What was going on here? Now that I felt better, I was beginning to worry. She'd looked fine in the library. Why wasn't she in school? At lunch I spotted Jason and Tanya talking, heads close together as if they were afraid someone would hear. I frowned. Then Vicky plopped down on the seat beside me, talking a mile a minute and I turned to listen.

The next day started much the same. The sun came up and I raced to get out of the house as soon as my mother left. Always afraid.

At school, the parking lot gleamed with fresh rain, a heavy fog hovered over the forest. It was so creepy...I shuddered and hurried to the door.

There was a silver car waiting in the driveway when I got home. I hopped out of the car—this time enthusiastically—and rushed into the house to greet my sister.

Tracy was waiting in the living room, as handsome as ever. Her auburn hair had grown long and wavy since I'd last seen her, and her eyes were deep blue. She was thin, and angular, with high cheek bones and a small nose. She looked like our Dad. He had been pretty too.

I squealed and hugged her. "How long have you been here?"

"I just pulled in." She laughed.

"Mom is going to be so psyched you're here. Tell me, tell me—how's college?"

We sat down on the couch while she filled me in on everything she'd been up to in the last three months. Tracy loved everything, as far as I could tell: her roommate, her teachers, her new friends. She did say she could do without all the extra homework. But she said it wasn't that difficult, just time consuming.

"What about you?" she asked, turning the conversation to me.

I told her about Jason and Marissa, and a lot of other things that were of little importance. I did not tell her about what had happened in the meadow, or ever since. As much as I loved my sister, and knew I could trust her, I also knew she'd be concerned. I was having a hard enough time as it was.

We got dinner started before Mom got home. When she came through the door she cried and squeezed my poor sister's face till it was beet red, saying how pretty she looked. And skinny.

"Haven't you been eating anything at all?"

Tracy turned her face to me and rolled her eyes. "Yes, Mom. Like a horse."

"Doesn't look like it to me."

My eyes kept wandering to the window. I tried to be discreet about it, but Tracy saw. She watched me with careful, shrewd eyes. I looked at the table and woofed down an enormous bite of spinach.

"Mom," Tracy said, still looking at me. "I'm going to take my things upstairs, now. Do you mind if I take Bethany with me?"

"Sure." The way my mom looked at me I wasn't surprised when she hastily agreed. I slunk out of the chair and followed my sister to the door.

We walked out in silence. I was about to pop the trunk when she caught my arm.

"What's going on with you?"

"Nothing." I tried to look offended.

"Oh whatever. You've been acting weird since I got here."

"I have *not*."

"No?" She lit a cigarette and leaned against the trunk of her car. "Spill it, kid. You're not going back in the house until you do."

As I glared at her she flipped down her shades and peeked up at the dark sky pointedly. I sighed.

"I'm waiting," she sang, picking at her nails.

"Remember that waterfall I showed you—right before you went to college?"

"The pretty one?"

"Yeah."

Tracy shrugged. "Sure, why?"

"Well—" I fidgeted with my hair. "I went for a walk down there a couple of days ago. And—I don't know, something was wrong. All of a sudden it got really quiet, and even though I was there for a long time and the sun was out, it was just....dead. And then I made it to the waterfall, and heard something, a twig snap. Maybe. And something ran away. I didn't really get to see it, but it was big....

"And then when I came home, someone was staring at me through my window. They were back this morning, I think, watching me. But I can't get a good look at them, because they move so fast...."I shook my head and shot her a look. Tracy's face was hard, she was staring off into the distance, clearly upset by what I had to say.

"And you didn't say anything to Mom about this?"

"Would you?"

She shook her head. I waited, but she didn't say anything. Her whole body was tense, though, as if she were expecting to see it, him—whatever, come out of the shadows at us.

"So what do I do?"

Tracy sucked on her cigarette. "I don't know. I'll think of something." She threw the cigarette down into the gravel and stepped on it hard, almost violently.

I thought about that. It made me feel better, knowing Tracy had my back.

"It's easier when I have to go to school," I admitted. "It feels better to be around people."

"Yeah..." I watched as she opened her trunk, she pulled out a little bag and strapped it over her shoulder. "C'mon, let's get this stuff inside."

I grabbed the other bag and lugged it out of the trunk. We brought them into the house, up the stairs. I was prepared to take them down to her old room, but Tracy surprised me by stopping at my door and going inside.

"Put the other bag there."

I dumped it in the corner.

"What are you doing?"

"I'm staying here." She rolled her eyes as if I should have known that already.

I sighed with relief. At least she didn't think I was crazy.

"Thanks, Trace."

She shot me a surprised look. "Don't sound so surprised, babe, it's what big sisters are for, you know."

I laughed.

"Can we stay up here, or will Mom worry?"

"Naw, she'll be fine. She's used to me hanging around by myself. Homework, you know."

Tracy made a face. "Geek."

"Hey!"

"Don't hey me, it's what you are. In two years you'll be like, the top nuclear scientist at the international lab or something.

"Seriously, though," she plopped down on the bed. "You should relax, you know? It's not a race."

"No. I get it."

"You okay?"

"Just a little freaked out is all."

"Hmmm." She sat up and put her hair in a ponytail. She looked tired. She sat there, staring at the floor for a long time.

"Maybe you should go to bed."

"Yeah, but I'm going to take a shower first."

She dug out some pajamas from one of her bags, and patted my shoulder on the way out. The room felt hollow, cold to me after she left. I squirmed, and pulled the cuffs of my shirt around my wrists uncomfortably.

The sun was going down, its final rays penetrating the window, and blinding my eyes. I turned away from it, half afraid of what I might see in the window. Eventually the stillness was just too much, and I went downstairs.

Mom was in her office, working. I heaved another sigh and headed to the kitchen. All this worrying was making me hungry. I dug through the refrigerator in search of something edible, eventually settling on an apple.

A tall form stood at the edge of the yard, partially concealed behind the trees. My heart gave a pang. I stared, but he didn't move. And I couldn't see his face. I heard a door slam, and Tracy sauntered in.

Slowly, then, he walked away. It didn't take long for my eyes to lose him in the trees.

Something in my chest stirred, began to throb.

"Bethany?"

I turned my huge, soccer ball sized eyes to her face.

She looked over her shoulder, towards mom's office, then came to my side. "Did you see something?" she whispered, leaning in so I could hear her. She wrung a towel in her hair as she spoke. I nodded weakly.

She dropped the towel and motioned towards the door with her head. I followed her silently, trying to be sneaky because I didn't want Mom to know. We slipped out onto the front porch. The night air was cool; it soothed the pulsing in my chest and allowed me to breathe again.

The grass was damp, our feet easily making trails. But when we got to the spot there was nothing to indicate where he'd stood. We stared at the spot, shocked.

"I don't understand."

Tracy didn't say anything, only pressed further back.

There, under the overbearing tamarack branches, were two very clear indentations. My breath caught, and I glanced around frantically.

He was nowhere to be seen.

I felt my sister's hand on my arm. She was looking in the same direction as I was, frowning.

"Do we call the cops?" I breathed.

"We should."

"Do you think they'd be able to do anything?"

"Did you see his face?"

"No."

"Probably not, then." She pulled back on my arm, and we slunk back into the house.

We went to bed early that night. I don't know why we did; we were both too edgy for sleep. As the night wore on, we were both watching the window carefully. Eventually, we dwindled off to sleep. I didn't know how long it was, but it seemed like right away I opened my eyes again.

And he was there. Only this time it was different. This was not the hideous stranger that had been following me since the day of the storm.

This was someone else. Someone who was more intent on what was going on in the forest, than at my window.

Slowly, I reached around to touch my sister's shoulder, keeping my eyes on the window.

He must have seen the motion in his peripheral vision. The form in the window turned his face to follow my motions with his eyes.

I squeezed her shoulder. I felt her move beside me, and then her face was level with mine.

And he was gone.

I exhaled in frustration.

Tracy groaned and shoved the hair out of her eyes. "What is it?" she demanded groggily. I lay back.

"Forget it, he's gone now."

Tracy dropped down on her belly and quickly picked up on her snoring routine. I watched the window for hours until the exhaustion finally overpowered me, and I had to sleep.

"Morning."

I groaned in response.

"Mom's shopping so don't expect any breakfast."

"I can feed myself you know."

She laughed. "Hey, did you try to wake me up last night?"

I nodded and sat up lazily. "Yeah. You missed him again, though. So I told you to go back to sleep." I told her what I saw, and she frowned.

"How come—"

I shook my head and rubbed my eyes. "Don't ask. I hardly get to see him, myself. He's too fast for me."

"Hmm." She finished combing her hair. "Well. I've been on red alert all morning, and I can tell you he hasn't been here."

"Good." I stood. "Maybe he figures he's scared us enough and is going to leave me alone from now on."

Tracy gave me a weird look—like she hoped I was right, but at the same time, knew that I wasn't.

I grabbed some clothes and went off to the bathroom. I changed quickly, without putting on any makeup. I just didn't feel like it today. After I was dressed, I found another apple in the fridge and took a bite, keeping my eyes from the window as I turned away. I didn't care to have any more adventures today.

Tracy glided down the stairs. She gawked at me.

"What!"

"Go put your make up on, kid. We're going out for a while."

I pouted.

Ten minutes later, she was dragging me out the front door.

"What. Are. We. Doing?"

"We're going to see where he went."

She lugged me to the spot where we'd found the footprints and released me. She stood, hands on her hips, staring out into the woods.

"Okay, Sherlock. Do you really think this is smart?"

Tracy shook her head. She turned her face to me and gave me a sneaky grin.

"No." She bit her lip. "But I do think that it might help."

"Help how?" I examined her face shrewdly. I in no way understood why I'd been forced to apply makeup for this.

"Well, the way I see it, the more we can tell the police, the more likely it is that they'll be able to help us."

"Like if we knew where he lives?"

"Or where he came from."

"You're insane."

She looked at me, hurt.

I turned a three-sixty and went for my car keys. "I'm going to the mall. Do you want to come with me or are you going to be too busy playing detective?"

"I suppose...."

"Good."

We didn't talk about it again, mostly because every time Tracy tried to steer the conversation in that direction, I cut her off. Saturday, and then Sunday went by without any more intrusion from my stalker. Tracy thought maybe we scared him away. I did not. This had happened before, and it didn't mean anything. But Tracy could only stay until Tuesday morning. When he didn't show up again, she figured I'd be all right.

Tracy had said goodbye to Mom that last night while I was in the shower. She woke me up early so we could have breakfast together before she had to go. This had been requested by me the night before. I didn't like the thought of her going away while I was comatose in bed. Who knows when she'd come to visit again? It was seven in the morning when she packed up her bags, and I helped her carry them to the car.

I waved as she pulled away, then turned and headed back inside. I grabbed the hair brush off the counter and started ripping it through my thick black hair as I went up to my room.

I stopped dead in the door way.

He wasn't there. The window was closed, and locked—the way we'd left it earlier.

Sitting on my pillow, was a full red rose.

My heart skipped a beat. Stark, cold fear rose up in my throat. I went over to the bed and touched the rose lightly. It was there, no illusion. I breathed a shuddering sigh and tried to get my bearings. I checked the windows, only to find nothing was unlocked or broken. How weird.

I picked up my bag from the floor and threw it over my shoulder. I still had the rose in my hand, though I didn't know why. I thrust everything into my car and hopped in. Instead of taking the normal way to school, I turned left on the trail and pulled over. I was going to be late. But I couldn't let this go on any longer. It had to end.

Funny, it used to be so beautiful to me. Now all I could sense was the toxic aura of danger in the air. I inhaled deeply and continued on my way; I had both the rose and the backpack with me—because I didn't trust the old man enough to leave my backpack there with money and my driver's license in it.

This was far dumber than anything Tracy could come up with, but that didn't matter. He had no right to be hanging around my house—much less be inside it. Whatever was going on I had had enough.

As I marched through the trees my anger began to ebb and with it, my courage. Everything scared me. The snaps of twigs under my feet were like mini explosions that never failed to send my heart into my mouth.

All this time I felt that unseen presence tagging behind me. Childlike.

Then I heard it. Someone had crunched on a branch, the breaking sound it made was very soft, and at first I wasn't sure I hadn't imagined it.

Did *I* do that?

No. I froze.

Leaves rustled somewhere in the distance. I looked back, not caring when I didn't see him. I knew he was there. The metallic pulsating reverberated through my chest. I said nothing—best to get to the waterfall first. My feet unfroze, carrying me closer to the meadow.

No.

I halted again, recognizing the voice—a memory that I could put neither a face nor a name to. I waited; when the voice didn't come again, I pressed on.

Bethany. The voice sharpened. Oh no. It was coming from my head! I was going crazy after all. *Turn around, Bethany. You don't want to do this.*

I shook my head. This couldn't be real.

Listen to me.

And I almost did, but then I remembered the rose in my hand; the ache in my chest grew into a raging inferno. I scowled. "No."

Before I knew what I was doing, I was plowing through the thick bushes.

In my head, the voice sighed.

The meadow was peaceful...in a disturbing way. The cedars and redwoods towered over my head, branches stretching out to reach the sun. Nothing had visibly changed. My hands tightened into fists. I forced myself to keep calm as I took in the sight. Something *had* changed. I could feel it in the air.

I told you not to come here, Bethany.

And you're making no sense, I retorted.

A splash in the river behind the trees caught my attention. But when nothing—no voice, nor face, nor body revealed itself I guessed it had just been a deer, running from my scent. My forehead knotted in frustration.

"Won't you just leave me alone!" I screamed into the forest.

The meadow proffered no answer. The trees swayed their graceful redwood arms in silence. Quietly mocking me.

I grunted, threw the rose down into the grass and stormed off. I marched through the trees; tripping on fallen branches and rocks. But that didn't stop me. I plowed through the rough pine needle walls and mazes of underbrush till I got to my car. I got to school late, of course. But I managed to make it to the second class of the day without getting caught.

Only one question kept my mind off everything else. I still had no idea what was going on. The more that went on, the more I doubted I had a regular run-of-the-mill stalker. Thinking about the voice made my eyes sting. I glared down at my notebook. I couldn't be crazy.

It was like I was part of some kind of horror movie.

Marissa materialized sometime during lunch. I didn't notice her till she waved Jason over. Tanya came to join the party, and entered in on the gossip that followed. I didn't listen.

Marissa hit me. "Hey, where were you this morning, anyway?"

"Hmm?"

"I said, where were you? I waited for you and everything."

"Oh. Uh, I was helping Tracy pack; she stayed over this weekend and had to leave early so...." It was almost true. I wasn't going to mention anything to them about Mr. Mystery Stalker. Tanya wasn't the only person I mistrusted lately.

After school was finally over, and I still hadn't been called in for strict and worthless punishment, I sauntered out into the humid, late day air. It smelled like rain. I took a deep breath and smiled. I'd always loved the smell of rain. For some reason it seemed to be the break in the clouds for me.

Then I reached my destination.

The rose was on the hood of my car.

My good mood vanished instantaneously. I tore the rose from the hood and threw it behind me, lurching myself into the car with enough force to make it rock.

Cold air blasted my face.

The rose had been placed neatly on top of my back pack. I stifled a groan.

Somewhere, I could have sworn I heard a man's laugh. I glimpsed out my window as a group of guys sauntered past.

Classmates. People I didn't know.

I turned my attention back to the rose.

It wasn't like other roses. I picked it up and twirled it between my fingers. The flower sparkled dimly in the light. Dark sparkles. The tips of the pointed petals were ebony. I lifted the flower to my nose, only to quickly toss it to the floor a second later.

It had smelled of death.

Tracy called that afternoon. I told her everything was fine. There was no sense in making her worry. I had a feeling that even if she were to turn around and come back, she would never be able to help me.

About two seconds after I hung up, the silence to became too much. So I went to Marcy's, a little bookshop in town. It was tiny, but homey—and it always smelled like coffee. Bookshelves lined the walls and filled the room. Off to the left side was a small set of brown leather furniture to match the dull rug. In the center was the cashier. I went in, forcing my eyes away from the strange orange sphere in the sky.

Gina looked up from the computer as I entered.

"Oh, hello, Bethany. What are you doing here so late?"

"Just looking..."

She grinned; her chubby cheeks nudged her glasses up off her face. She pointed to the short bookshelf on my left.

"Our new releases are there," she told me.

"Thanks."

When I left, I had three more books to read. It was pretty late, but I didn't think Mom would be home until midnight or after, so I didn't hurry. I drove slowly down the streets, dreading what I might see when I pulled into the driveway.

My headlights caught nothing. The house was still. Dark. Just the way I'd left it. My heart thudded, and when I slammed my car door shut, the sound made me jump. I hurried to the front door, unlocked it, and threw myself inside, locking it again immediately.

I got ready for bed and crawled in, bringing the first of my new books with me. Interesting as it was, it couldn't distract me from my trepidation. I flashed a glance at the window from time to time nervously, waiting for the full moon to come into the frame of my window. Hoping that by some miracle, it had paled in the time I'd refused to look at it. Somewhere, in my mind, I knew that was illogical, but the rest of me didn't want to know that.

CHAPTER FIVE

I t had been red.

I'd been stuck in Spanish for half an hour, but I wasn't learning anything.

The moon had been red. Like the rose, only it hadn't sparkled. I just couldn't get used to it. It was like there was this black fog hanging over my head, and I didn't understand it. It terrified me.

And yet, now more than ever, I was starting to feel something else—intrigued. I knew the police couldn't come help me now because there was a good chance I'd never have enough proof. And I knew that if I told my mom, she would freak out and probably never let me walk out the front door again. Marissa might not even believe me. Tracy couldn't save me. I was alone.

Part of me wished that things would go back to normal. That part of me wanted normalcy so badly sometimes it felt like I was actually losing my mind.

And in my heart, I knew things would never be the same as they were before the first fateful night, when the blood red moon showed me its face.

Relief freed my lungs to breathe again once I pulled into the driveway. I sighed, glad to see the end of the day. I hesitated a moment after I turned off the engine, eyes scanning the shadows. I slipped out of the car and headed up the walk, keeping my gaze on the tree line.

A man stood at the corner of my house, watching me with dark, threatening eyes. I flinched.

"What do you want?"

"Someone wants to speak with you, Bethany."

"No." The bubble in my chest made it hard for me to inhale. I gasped and shrank back.

"Don't make this hard, girl."

"No. I'm not going anywhere with you," I insisted, panic making me sound pathetic. I backed up until I touched the hard metal of my car door. I glared up at him. His arm shot out; I flinched, anticipating the pain that was coming.

Something strange happened. A dark form dashed out from the trees. It collided with the man with a loud thud......

And then they both were gone.

My heavy breathing was the only sound in the stillness. My knees gave in beneath me. Why had he saved me? I was certain he was the man I'd seen in the lawn the day Tracy stayed over, the one watching the forest. The other one....I shuddered, remembering his face in my window.

They weren't human. Of that I was completely sure.

I clasped my shaking hands together, pressing them to my forehead. What could I do?

I sat there for hours, trying to figure that out. The only thing I could think of was to go back to the forest, where this had all started. Horror filled me at the thought, but I ignored it. My mind was made up. I would go.

We had another half day, the day after I'd almost been kidnapped—no storm this time, just a half day to give everyone a break, which was cool, but it wasn't normal. I didn't take the time to wonder what'd forced the school officials' hands on that one, and I didn't really care so long as I was free.

I took my time getting to the forest, dawdling and taking alternate routes because I could. The closer I got, the more my hands shook. I wanted to turn around and go back. Home. Where it was safe. I was glad that the voice didn't come back. For once it was normal, self-preservation talking. And I was having a hard time believing it hadn't been someone else before.

Home wasn't safe anymore, anyway, I argued with myself. If anything, I could at least get to the bottom of this mess here.

The forest greeted me, and not without its normal serenity. That was a good sign. Still, I bit my lip, and hesitated. I wasn't sure about this. I remembered the voice and its warning, and almost turned around. I could see the waterfall ahead of me, dropping down gallons of icy water into the pool beneath it. The sound was soothing.

And menacing.

I walked over to the embankment, ignoring my fear. I tried to tell myself that I was doing the smart thing. Instead of being the victim, I was taking my fate into my own hands. I was being brave...

But I felt so stupid.

A group of birds flew by; my head snapped around to see what had scared them. The branches of a tall tree were swinging back and forth, as though someone had been holding them back, but was now gone. I tucked my hair behind my ear and plopped down by the water. My senses were on the alert, waiting. Something must be coming soon.

I stared down into the glassy water, trying to calm myself. Force myself to stay. I dipped my hand into the water, breaking up the mirror-like smoothness. I fished my hand around, watching my face distort and change. A smiled touched my lips, and the eyes in the water danced. Green eyes—cat's eyes, as my father used to say.

Then I saw something else in the water. A reflection of something.

It was hard to see at first, it was just dark. My fear made it impossible to turn around. So I stopped stirring the water. I waited, and the form eventually took shape. A tall man in dark jeans and a t-shirt was standing behind my shoulder. His hair was short and wavy, and his pretty slanted eyes were deep blue. I turned. He was beautiful. And with a pang, I realized that I hated him.

He didn't speak. His face was brooding, weary; he put his hands in his pockets and looked away from me.

"Well"— I snapped.

His head jerked up, as though he'd forgotten I was there. "You were here last week."

I nodded. "I usually am," I replied, irritated by the insinuation. I belonged here more than he did. "*You've* been to my house."

The man smiled wryly. "Yes, I usually am." There was sourness in his tone.

I squinted at him, my lips twitching downwards. This couldn't be the man I'd been afraid of.

He sat in front of me. "I didn't have any other choice." The way he spoke made me think about the monster that had tried to kidnap me.

My lips parted, intending to ask him about what had happened, but he stiffened. His eyes locked on something behind my shoulder, hatred turning his cool blue eyes hard. I turned.

Fingers dug into my sides and strong arms gripped me around the waist; the ground flew out from under me. I was swung around and placed firmly on the grass behind him.

Disoriented, I peeked over his shoulder, to see a dark figure step out of the forest line. And, though he too was beautiful, there was an aura about him that disturbed me. I frowned.

"Problem?"

My protector smiled a little bit as he glimpsed at me. "Uh-hmm." He turned his eyes then to meet his enemy's, his chin raised arrogantly. "I didn't expect you to find your way here so soon, Darrell."

Darrell spread his hands. "What? You think too little of me." He stopped, about ten feet from where we stood. The man before me tensed as Darrell's dark eyes drifted over to me. Horrible, wicked eyes. They made me think of the stalker. I shuddered away.

"Who is this?" he pointed, his voice betraying his sarcasm.

"That's none of your business."

Darrell bridled. "Erik," he pronounced my protector's name patronizingly. "You know everything you do has an interest to me. If you've found an alliance...I have a right to know." He shrugged with one shoulder and smiled.

"You have a right to nothing."

I spoke up, demanding to know what was going on.

Darrell cocked his head to the side. "Bethany does not know?"

How did he know my name? I swallowed once. He was toying with the man before me. Asking who I was when he really knew...probably everything.

"She hasn't entered my confidence."

"Then why protect her?"

I could feel the exasperation build up inside of Erik. This wasn't going well. All the frigid small talk was part of something else. A pretense. I sensed the livid emotions emitting from Erik and wondered why he bothered.

I thought I saw someone standing at the edge of the fringe of the meadow, but it disappeared as soon as I saw it. I grimaced, and my heart began to throb heavily, suffocating me.

"Because I have a respect for life—unlike you," I heard Erik reply.

Darrell laughed at him. "You always were the soft one of the family." He took a languid step closer. Erik reached back, turning sideways, so his arm was around my waist and he was half-facing me. This time I was certain I saw someone watching from the sinuous vegetation.

We were surrounded.

Darrell made a quick motion with his hand, and, from all around us, stalked out of the brushes a dozen or so men.

Erik pulled me in closer.

My heart pounded in my throat, turning my knees into mush. It'd been a mistake to come here.

Now I wasn't going to get back out of it.

Darrell stood motionless as they came at us. He seemed to be enjoying this, somehow. Taking pleasure in the fact that he'd taken Erik by surprise.

Yet, as the first white haired man reached us, Erik struck him hard with his free hand. He flew backwards into the water.

Erik knocked a couple of men back, as he did with the first, but more came in and grabbed him by the arms and dragged us apart so that I was no longer protected. A pair of hands shoved me down to the ground, and I instantly recognized the horrible face from the parking lot. I struggled to push him away, trying and wishing that I could scream for help, but I couldn't make a sound. I couldn't even breathe.

Erik fought with them, trying to get close to me again. The man that had tackled me, rushed over to help them. I realized they weren't going to let him leave the meadow alive.

And they were going to take *me*.

A soldier with hollow cheeks grasped my arms and jerked them behind me as he pulled me to my feet. I struggled with him, pressure building up in my chest again. I caught Erik's eyes as the wicked man dragged me away.

He was trying. But he couldn't save me; I had to fend for myself, at least for now.

The bubble of energy formed in my chest, I felt it vibrate, and expand until it exploded. My arm, acting on its own, whipped back. The force of my blow sent my enemy reeling. He was soon replaced by another; I balled up my fists and bashed him in the chest with enough force to crush his ribcage.

The sound of running feet had me jumping up into the air, in an aerial back flip. Landed on my knees.

Darrell was staring at me, looking more surprised that I felt. I grinned at him from my crouching position. Ready when they came at me again.

Erik tackled the monster that had tried to kidnap me. We didn't have to say anything for me to know he was smug.

I heard a weapon swinging through the air; I flipped over backwards, landing—on my feet this time—behind him. When he spun around, I smashed him in the face with my fist.

Another man grasped my arm; and I booted that one in the midsection. Someone came at me from the other side. I hit him in the face with my elbow then Erik clobbered him on the skull. He dropped.

We weren't paying attention.

I was backtracking, trying to find some place where the crowd wasn't so bad.

Erik on the other hand, was right in the middle of it. I couldn't tell what he felt more—anger or entertainment.

I couldn't think of things like that now. No time.

I faced the next soldier that came towards me. I kicked him neatly under the chin and prepared for the next attack.

But it didn't happen. The next attack did not come. I looked around, puzzled.

The meadow was empty. Only Erik was standing in the center of the meadow, some thirty yards from me with his hands in his pockets. He looked like he was laughing.

I dropped my fists. I walked over, cautiously. But my legs were numb underneath me, and I collapsed. Erik caught me around the waist.

I looked up into his deep blue eyes; tried hard to retain my anger, to demand answers. But his face was so ridiculously handsome, all that came out was a weak, "You have to tell me."

"I know. Come on, let's go. It's getting late."

We were quiet for a moment. "What do you want to know first?" Now that the excitement was over, Erik was wary. There were things he didn't want me to know.

"What does he want?"

"You."

I didn't understand. "I don't have anything to do with the two of you."

Erik smirked. "Not technically."

"What's that supposed to mean?"

Erik sighed. "It means that even though you never knew my brother and I existed, we were not so ignorant of you. I've been watching you, and so has he. He's been waiting."

I took a step away from him. "Waiting for...."

"You were born with an extraordinary talent, Bethany. One that, if used by the wrong side, could kill many—" He paused, his eyes searched my face. "People."

"I think you got the wrong girl."

"That's impossible."

We walked along, neither of us speaking. I didn't want to believe this. Not any of it.

"How long have you been watching me?" I asked. Erik hesitated. Apparently, this was one of the questions he'd been hoping I wouldn't ask. "How long?"

He looked down at the path. "Since the day you were born....or thereabouts."

CHAPTER SIX

I gawked at the serene face before me. He couldn't be that much older than me.

It was impossible.

"That's not true. I don't believe you." I ran my hand through my hair.

"It's true," he assured me quietly. His eyes were deep, undeceiving.

"It's not *possible*!"

"There was a time, I believe, when you thought it was also impossible for someone to run at seventy or eighty miles an hour."

My thoughts flew back to that day in the driveway, when he'd saved me. How incredibly *fast* he'd been. I shook my head. "How?"

"You'll find out in time."

We were at the door now. I paused, uncertain if I should let him in. Curiosity won out over mistrust, however, and I led him into the living room. He sat down in the chair by the window; I placed myself on the sofa, across the room.

I told him that I wanted to know how it'd all started.

Erik told me how, growing up, his brother was cruel to him, and the servants; how his behavior had forced their father to throw him out. In retaliation, Darrell had poisoned the king's wine. The attempt failed. And that's when Erik's mother made the decision that was to start a war.

"She knew that if Darrell took the throne, our world would literally go up in flames. It's long been the custom of our kingdom that the eldest of the family is to take the place of the parents when they die. Mother amended that. And when she died, I was crowned the next evening." Erik stared out the window, pensive. "Things got out of hand. Darrell and his band of rebels interrupted the ceremony and tried to take the palace. They were driven out, though of course that never discouraged him. Darrell's men are from the very annals of the empire, the lowest of the low..... They can do enormous damage, despite their small numbers. If Darrell had been able to use you the whole kingdom would've been lost in a day."

"Sounds like you have a fight on your hands." I paused, running my hands along the couch cushions. "Look, I don't know what you seem to think I can do for you. But whatever it is, I don't think I'm up to it. And I don't want to be involved."

"There's more to you than you think, trust me."

I grunted.

"Don't you remember what you did in the meadow, Bethany?"

I frowned at him. "I'm trying to forget that, actually." Then something occurred to me. "Wait. You said your *world* is in danger?"

"I said that, yes."

"You're not, like, an alien or anything, right?"

He laughed. "I guess you could say that. But most people just call my kind fairies."

The blood froze inside me. Fairies.

Didn't Mom say something about them? I tried but couldn't remember now. I did, however, remember the moon last night......

His eyes were bright. "Don't worry. We have time. Get used to the idea, ask questions, it's fine with me."

"Won't they need you?"

He shook his head. "No, I don't think so. Not yet anyway."

"Will Darrell come back?"

Erik nodded. "He might."

I didn't like the sound of any of this. "If you've been watching over me for so long, then how come that freak was posted outside my window every night?"

"It takes time to cross between my world and yours, Bethany."

I grunted again.

"He was there to make sure you weren't already my ally, and to keep me away from you. Obviously he didn't succeed"—

I stopped listening to him then. I went to the kitchen, feeling his eyes on the back of my head. I needed to think.

I GOT READY FOR BED that night quickly. I wondered if I was making another mistake by letting Erik talk me into this. Of course, I really didn't have a choice—I was a part of it now whether I wanted to be or not. Worse. I'd been recruited just by existing. There was no escape for me.

Before I went to sleep, I sat at my window and drew back the curtain. The moon was red. My breathing stopped.

Erik was there, he was looking at the moon too, a look of somber recollection on his beautiful face. Our eyes met, then I let the curtain fall back into place. I crawled into bed and pulled the blankets up around my chin. As long as he was there, nothing would bother me tonight, I was sure.

Everything I knew was about to change. I could feel it, and I didn't like the sensation—like I had fallen into an ever-deepening abyss that I'd never be able to crawl back out of.

I didn't go to school. As soon as Mom went to work, Erik showed up in my living room. I jumped slightly, spilling coffee on myself and the floor.

"Don't people knock where you're from?" I demanded.

He laughed. "Occasionally."

I growled under my breath as I mopped up the coffee. "You want coffee?" I asked, not looking at him. I was still trying to get the stain out of my sweater.

"No."

I gave up and went to curl up on the couch. "So I have another question."

"Go ahead."

"Why didn't you just tell me everything when we were in the meadow the other day?"

Erick raised his eyebrows. "That wasn't me. I hadn't made it to the meadow yet."

"You mean..." I felt the blood drain from my head.

"I tried to stop you. When I couldn't, I had him chased off, and went to your house to make sure you were all right. I hung around, though, thinking that maybe I could find a way to end everything right then and there but that never happened. Obviously."

That explains the voice, I thought, relieved that my mind hadn't defaulted yet.

Something Erik was thinking bothered him. His face turned a shade darker. A shade meaner. I almost asked what was wrong, but I wasn't sure I wanted to find out.

Thunder crashed in the distance, and I shot a look at the dark sky.

"I don't know what to tell you," I confessed finally. I shouldn't have to help him. I didn't even know him.

Erik didn't say anything. I glanced back, and he was looking at me sadly. "You don't have to say anything right now. I don't want you to choose too soon. What I'm asking you to do is very dangerous, and really, I have no right to ask."

I thought about that for a moment. It was not like he was a normal person, asking for a normal favor. He made it very clear that I could die in his world. His brother was stalking me, and even though Erik said he was trying to protect me I didn't imagine that was going to help much after a while. There was simply too much on his plate for him to look out for me all the time.

I'd been caught up in this, I realized again, just by living. Maybe a choice didn't have to be made. Maybe there was none to make.

I'd always thought of fairies as a figment of someone's imagination—stories for grandmas to tell their grandbabies. I'd never actually believed in them.

Which made all this very hard to accept.

And I knew that, by anyone's standards Erik would be considered insane. I'd have thought so myself, but after everything that had taken place lately, the only explanation that made sense was that he was telling the truth—not just what he believed to be the truth, but that it was the for real, naked truth.

I sighed. "I wonder if Darrell watched me, too. Since the day I was born," I murmured, to distract myself.

"No."

"Hmmm....." I stared out the window; watched as the rain fell against the glass. I didn't hear when Erik left. I didn't move from that spot for hours, and Mom worried that evening when I didn't eat dinner. I just told her I wasn't feeling well and went upstairs for the rest of the night.

CHAPTER SEVEN

I didn't have a lot of time to think it over. I went back to school for the sole reason I wanted to be around people. I had to escape to a normal world, even for a little while. No matter how mundane.

Thoughts of what I'd seen and heard made it difficult for me to pay attention. I even snapped at Marissa a couple of times. I knew I should feel bad about that. But all my emotions were tied up, and I couldn't feel anything.

Erik showed up in the parking lot after school, his face was strained. My heart paused for a moment. Something had happened.

He told me Darrell was on the move. Word was he had an operation of some kind in motion. Erik didn't know what it was yet. But he had to go back. There was no more time; was I willing?

"I really don't think I have a choice," I said. I smiled at him unhappily.

Erik grimaced at me. "Yes you do." He wasn't going to make this decision an easy one for me.

I hesitated. The cool breeze whistled by, blowing a few strands of hair into my face. I pushed them behind my ear. "I'm in."

Erik grinned at me, and reached for my keys.

"Where are we going?"

"Back to the waterfall."

I gulped. "Yeah. You know, I'm not really that anxious to get back....."

He made a face. "You said you were in....We have to leave now."

We were at the waterfall in a matter of minutes. Erik led me to the meadow in silence. I could think of nothing to say, far too nervous to attempt conversation. Once we reached the meadow, he turned to me. "Give me your hand."

Suddenly it was like the world around me was slipping away, and I was being ripped from it. It shuddered and swayed with glistening pale veils. My heart beat faster. I could feel myself moving—very quickly—up and out of the meadow.

Erik's hand held me sturdy, but it offered little comfort since I was now torn between our two worlds in mid-air. Or at least, that's what it felt like. When it stopped, I opened my eyes.

We'd landed in a tree.

Erik let go of me and hopped down. I stared down at him, shocked. He had landed some thirty feet down, somehow unharmed.

At least, I didn't think he'd been harmed. I couldn't really see him. I grasped onto the nearest limb and began to hyperventilate.

"Jump!" I heard him call up to me.

My head shake was jerky; I nearly fell off the limb. "N-no wa-ay!"

"Bethany." He sounded irritated. "It's the only way down. Come on."

A high-pitched squeal whispered between my lips, I think it was supposed to be a scream. I bit my lip and dared to look down. Overpowering dizziness swept over me and I swayed backwards.

My heart panged electrically, and my fingers tightened around the branch. I squeezed my eyes shut. I clutched the tree limb in my hands without even the slightest intention of letting go.

"I'll catch you!" Erik told me.

"I'll die!" I screamed back, without looking down.

"Bethany!"

"NO!"

The limb I was perched on started to quake. I clung to the branch and hugged myself closer to it. The shaking got rougher.

And then I was falling.

When the movement stopped, I opened my eyes to see Erik's face smiling above mine. My eyes narrowed. "You made me fall."

"*You* weren't going to come down." He shrugged.

Erik put me down. I followed him reluctantly as he led the way through the forest once more.

It was nothing like the one I'd left behind. I soaked in the tranquil beauty almost happily. Blue seemed to have replaced green as the flora color of choice here. Only the grass and ferns retained their natural—well, natural to me—color.

Flowers blanketed the ground, all of them shimmered brightly in even the dimmest light. So much like the meadow in my dream.

From a tree beside me, I plucked a leaf. A combination of three leaves with points curling up out of the center of the collaboration...up close it looked like a flower.

"Hm." I turned the leaf around, analyzing it. I realized then that Erik had gotten quite far ahead of me. I dropped my discovery and ran to catch up to him.

We walked for miles, neither of us speaking. And then we broke through the forest line and a small village met our eyes. I started walking straight ahead.

Hands grabbed me by the arms and dragged me backwards.

"What do you think you're doing?" I demanded.

"Wait." Erik's eyes searched the streets for a long time, then he let his hand drop. "Okay." But he was stiff, waiting for trouble.

I freed myself from the clingy burrs and stumbled out onto the street. There were many more houses than I had thought. And they were all very large, with their front doors wide open. I spent some time trying to peek—to see how these people lived, but Erik informed me that even here that's considered rude. I had to admit to myself, I felt a surge of vengeful delight when he said that and hoped someone saw me with him—served him right for shaking me out of a monster tree.

We reached a large, rectangular house. A makeshift restaurant packed with a ton of people. All of which were tall, like Erik, and lean with small features.

He pushed me over to the bar. Where there were a bunch of three-legged chairs in front of it. "I must talk with one of my generals. Stay here."

I took a chair, automatically, and nodded. I didn't look at him, though, not having forgiven him yet. He sighed. "I'll be back soon."

A young woman with stringy dark hair stepped up as he left, her eyes following him worshipfully. "So," she began, and I lifted my eyes. "You know our majesty..." She looked down her nose at me. I felt the eyes of the entire room on my back. I folded my arms on the counter, wondering whether or not I should correct her mistake. I *didn't* know Erik. Not well anyway. "What's a human doing mingling with a fairy king, hmm?"

The insinuation stung; I glared at her for a long moment. "What's your name?"

"Victoria."

"Victoria," I nodded once, committing it to memory. "I don't see how that's any of your business."

"What are you, some kind of spy?"

"No. However, I'd be careful about what you say to me, Victoria, I may just be the only thing standing between your bar and Darrell's soldiers."

As soon as I said it, I realized I shouldn't have. The silence was crushing; I could feel the icy looks of the customers on my back, but I didn't take my eyes off of her face.

Erik touched my arm. "We're done here." His face was cold. I got off the chair, no longer resisting his hold on my arm as he led me to the doors.

"What were you *thinking*? Humans are not looked well upon here. Don't you know that already? Don't you listen to the stories?"

Now he was being too funny. "I never wanted to be here. Don't forget that you're the one that got me into this, Erik."

He chortled arrogantly, looking at the trees. "Please. Don't remind me."

"Does it embarrass you, then?" I stopped in the middle of the glassy gold-pink street.

"Don't make a scene. We'll discuss this when we get back to the palace."

"No. I want to know."

"Bethany"—

"NO."

Erik bit his lip and stalked over to me slowly. "*Don't* make a fool out of me." He snatched my arm and dragged me across the empty town. He let me go once we reached the field. I followed him till the village was out of sight, then dropped down on the ground, crossing my arms and legs like Pocahontas.

It took Erik a while to notice I wasn't following. But when he did, he charged up the hill like an angry bear.

"I do not appreciate the way I'm being treated."

"Bethany, I'm sorry. But you have to"— He didn't sound sorry. Not even a little.

I scowled at him. "I don't have to do anything. It's not my world that's at stake here, Erik, it's yours. And I'm not interested in saving it, if I'm going to be treated like dirt the entire time I'm here. So I suggest, that you rethink your attitude, your *highness*."

Erik stared at me blankly. I was probably the first person in the world to talk to him like that. Maybe it'd do him some good.

He sat down next to me. "Bethany, I'm sorry, believe me. I don't want you to feel like you don't belong here—you do. You weren't even supposed to know—that's really the only village that thinks that way. As a matter of fact, there's one city totally convinced that humans are a higher race than fairies. Really." He raised his eyebrows, and stared at me intently, willing me to believe him.

I felt my heart warm in response and looked away. I didn't want to forgive him just yet.

"I can assure you everyone else in the kingdom will treat you well." Erik fidgeted with a piece of hay. "Of course, that was my fault back there. I shouldn't have left you alone with them. But I had to speak to Jonathon. I didn't want him to meet you because he talks too much."

"So." I stopped. "Are we okay now? No more fighting?"

"Absolutely. Just try to open up your ears a bit, Bethany. I seriously don't want you to get killed."

I made a face. Erik took my hand and helped me off the ground. We continued on our way. I couldn't see anything that resembled a palace anywhere near here, only miles and miles of plains and huge hills. Beyond that were mountains I hoped we wouldn't climb.

"So what else don't I know?"

"Well." He pointed south. "In that direction lies the fortress Darrell built." He smirked. "I sent an army to destroy it; it's been burning for months."

I raised my eyebrows.

"To the east," he pointed again, "is the city of Geist. The biggest city in the entire empire. Fairies there are drawn by the river. Since stories say that the water from it will give immortality to those that drink it." He rolled his eyes.

"You don't believe the stories?"

"They're old fables, like the kinds you heard from your grandmother and grandfather."

I remembered he'd been watching me my whole life with a tiny shock. "So," I said, so he wouldn't notice my reaction. "Fairies can't live forever, then."

Erik shook his head. "We live and die—just as you do." He looked down at me and grinned. "It just takes longer."

"How old are you?"

"Old enough."

"Is that the only answer you're going to give me?"

He chortled. "I've been around longer than your mother, let's just leave it at that."

I thought about that. Then, "So how does it work?"

"How does what work?"

"This." I held my arms out wide and twirled around. "How's it work? The sun, the moon, the years, tides....Is it all like home? Well. Obviously not. But kind of?" I looked at him cocking my head to the side and brushing the hair out of my eyes.

Erik shook his head. "No. Not really.

"We're part of a different universe completely. Our world is round like yours, but its millions times larger, and as for the sun...." He looked up. "We haven't figured that out yet. We count our years by the moon. It's different for every 'month' we count to seven, and we have a year. But the moon doesn't follow us around, like yours does with earth. And we have four."

I frowned. "If that's the case then maybe you have four suns as well."

He shrugged. He really didn't seem to care about that.

We were still walking. To the best of my knowledge, we had a long, long way to go yet. I stumbled ahead of him, walking backwards and surveying the view in front of me.

"To the north?"

"That's where the palace is."

"Is that all?" I watched him skeptically. There had to be more than just that.

"Of course not. Forests, a few small villages, the mountains. *Obviously....*"

My bangs got in my eyes again, I shook them away and turned around. The mountains seemed bigger now. "I hope we're not going to climb them."

"No. We can go around them."

I thought about that, how long it would take, then I realized—I'd forgotten all about Mom and Tracy. I asked him how long it would be before I could go home.

"That's not going to be a problem."

"But"—

"No buts. Everything's going to be fine. Trust me."

I stopped arguing. There was no way I was going to convince him otherwise but I was sure I'd be coming home to a disaster zone.

The going was smooth, at first. The further we went, however, the more inclined the ground became. I was exhausted; I wondered why he didn't just super-speed us to the palace. I peeked at him out of the corner of my eye; he was looking straight ahead, lost in his thoughts.

I took another step, my foot landed on something soft. It lashed out at my legs, hissing loudly. I screamed and fell back; my butt hit the ground hard. The snake rose up, its thick neck and head flattened out; it came at me, its mouth open wide, sharp fangs jutting out...I screamed again.

Erik's boot came down on its head hard; I had no doubt, after the sickening sound it made, that he had killed it.

I got up, my stomach recoiling, and exhaled. I was shaking all over, my knees felt like jelly under me.

Erik watched me; he grinned in a mockingly. "Afraid of snakes?"

"You didn't know that?" I leaned on my knees.

"I must've missed that part."

I pouted. "Let's go," I snapped.

I tried to calm myself, breathing deeply as I walked. Erik followed behind me. I didn't look back at his face, to see the amusement I knew was there.

CHAPTER EIGHT

By late afternoon, the plains were behind us. In the distant valley, a few peaked rooftops poked up out the nothingness. Erik took a hold on my arm and led me into the trees. I opened my mouth to ask him why, but the look on his face made me close it again quickly. He grabbed me around the waist. We glided quickly through the shimmering blue forest.

We approached from the east, rushing towards the sultry air that surrounded the village. It smelled of hot metal and burning vegetation. At the edge of the forest, Erik stopped. He put me down.

I heard it. The sound of clinking chains and screams. Appalled, I looked up at Erik. His handsome face was livid, his hands knotted up into fists. My heart turned over; at first I thought it was because of the fear.

Something else was wrong.

"Wait here."

No, I wanted to say. I didn't want to be left alone here; I couldn't speak. Smoke from the village rolled through the trees. It burned my eyes and throat. I coughed. The action sent a sudden, searing pain through my body. Like angry claws were tearing me apart from the inside out.

"Bethany?"

I tried to speak. To tell him. Something was wrong. What was happening? Fear made me dizzy.

Thick smoke filled my mouth, forced its way down my throat. I coughed again, and sunk to my knees. I couldn't breathe. The smoke was smothering me. What little oxygen I could get fed the fire in my lungs; it grew and grew until I thought for certain my whole body must be on fire.

Instantly, he had me off the ground, my face pressed against his shoulder. He ran rapidly, faster than an Olympian. I only knew when we were away from the village when I could no longer hear the fairies screaming.

I couldn't open my eyes. I wanted to tell him to put me down, to help them instead but I couldn't find the strength in me to say it. I choked, and coughed. My limbs trembled uncontrollably. Was I going to die then?

Through the tunnel, I heard Erik's voice. "Are you all right?" The air smelled clean; but I still couldn't breathe right. I struggled to clear my throat. I thought I heard him murmur something like "so much for that idea."

"I'm okay," I grumbled. "Put me down."

"Bethany, you can't breathe."

I tried to take a deep breath. It stabbed in my lungs, but at least it was getting down in there. My head swam.

Somehow, I managed to tell him what I wanted.

"No."

"E-Erik..."

He wasn't listening to me. I tried to protest, but deep down I knew I wasn't doing myself any good. The more I talked the worse I sounded, the dizzier I became. And I had a terrible nagging feeling that I wasn't thinking straight. I let my head rest against his chest. Within the next several hours, we had reached the palace.

"Your"— I heard someone say. The voice sounded far away, though rationally I knew the speaker was probably quite near.

"Don't waste my time," Erik snapped. "She breathed in the smoke down at Kynig."

"Oh my..." The man sounded frightened.

"I forgot. I didn't think it would have this kind of effect."

Erik was moving again. I felt something hard and bulky press against my back. I opened my eyes, glad now that he hadn't let me walk.

The fire in my lungs was worse, shooting its way up through my chest and throat now. I whimpered.

Then the man entered my line of vision, he was looking at me skeptically, a prominent frown on his chubby face.

"Don't just stand there, man." Erik's tone was hard. The doctor jumped.

"Yes, yes, of course." He turned to a tall white table covered in small silver vials. He picked one up and studied it carefully. "How much did she inhale?"

"Too much—she says her lungs feel like her lungs are on fire."

"Hmm."

My lungs convulsed; I gasped wildly, started to sit up so I could breath. Erik pushed me down again, and put a hand on my forehead.

"Don't," he murmured softly.

"Is-s"—I tried to speak, but Erik put his hand over my mouth.

The doctor quickly opened the vial. He shoved past a girl that tried to hold out a spoon-like utensil to him. "Don't be a fool, child. She's going to take the whole bottle."

Together, he and Erik propped me up; they poured the sour, acidic medicine down my throat. I hated every second of it; the medicine made the fire burn hotter, but I couldn't fight them. I was too tired. Too weak.

When they were done, I curled over on my side and closed my eyes. My body ached. I tried to concentrate on something other than the pain. The medicine already churned sickeningly inside my stomach.

Wonderful.

I didn't want to think about my discomfort, so I tried—fought—to focus on the soothing sound of Erik's voice.

"Is she going to be okay?"

"She should be fine." But the doctor sounded uncertain. "How long was she in the smoke for?"

"About ten minutes."

"Hmm."

"I didn't think of it, really."

"You wouldn't. Darrell's army is burning old homes, ancient painting and the like. They shouldn't. It's releasing toxins into the air. Not enough to harm any of us yet. But definitely enough to kill one of her kind."

Erik sighed heavily.

"I'm sure she'll be fine, Your Majesty."

It was quiet. My body felt like lead; I took a deep, painful breath and tried to relax. Then someone covered me with a blanket and I fell asleep not long after.

I woke up a little better than I'd been before. But weaker. It was hard to open my eyes, and when they did open I found that I was alone. I forced myself to look around, noting the shelves stacked with bottles and other medical equipment—it was like the guy was a doctor, a scientist, and a pharmacist all rolled into one.

My eyes closed. I made them open again. I heard footsteps, and the doctor entered the room. He was studying a piece of paper attentively. I wondered what it was, but I didn't care, I just wanted him to give me something to make the pain stop.

He looked up and smiled. "You're awake." He sounded overjoyed.

"Uhhmn...."

He held up a hand. "Don't bother. You're very weak right now, dear. You need to sleep."

But I didn't want to sleep. I tried again. It sounded like I was groaning.

Somehow he knew what I meant. "He'll be here, don't worry." He grinned. "He hasn't abandoned you."

When? I wanted to ask. But I couldn't. I slipped back into sleep. When I opened my eyes again, Erik was there. He was speaking with the doctor. I watched them for a moment, gauging my strength. Then I tried to sit up.

"Whoa! Now." He was there, pushing me down.

This time I could speak. Kind of. "I don't....want to lie down."

Erik cocked his head to the side. "What do you want to do, then? Run a marathon? Bethany, you're sick."

I huffed. "But"—I said, my voice rough. Fighting with the doctor was making me tired, my lungs were starting to burn again. I lay back, then, afraid the pain was going to start. It didn't, just stayed a dull, burning ache in my chest. I swallowed, trying to squelch the sensation.

"She seems to be doing better," Erik observed, sounding pleased.

"She won't be if she keeps this up."

"Erik..."

"A few more days, Bethany. Then you can do as you please."

"I hate you."

"Hating me won't help you get out of here." We frowned at each other from across the room. The good doctor was looking from me to Erik as though he couldn't believe his ears. Maybe I'd been right in the field the other day, I felt the beginning of a smile curl around my lips. Erik ignored him and went to sit next to me.

"Well...can you at least...tell me what happened back...there?"

"Darrell's army took over that village a week ago. They've been tearing everything apart and burning it—just for the destruction, I think they aren't burning anything *useful*. Just burning it. Some of the houses are very old—hundreds, thousands of years old—apparently material they've been burning is releasing poisonous vapors into the air." He dropped his head into his hands. "I'm sorry, I didn't know. I've been there before, many have, the toxins have never affected anyone the way they did you."

"But I'll be okay, right?"

He was surprised. "Of course you will. Why wouldn't you?"

I motioned to the doctor with my hand. "He didn't sound hopeful...."

"No. And I didn't *feel* hopeful. The way you were looking, I thought for sure you were going to die before I got you here." He shook his head. "That'll never happen again."

"You didn't know," I tried to comfort him.

"I should have."

"What happened to them?"

Erik knew what I meant. He nodded his head slightly as he spoke. "After I got you here safely my men and I took care of it. We've also been evacuating a city near the Auyen plains. Darrell's soldiers moved in there while I was gone." He shook his head angrily. "I can't believe Mia didn't send the army in before...Now we have to stop him before he does too much damage. The Auyen cities are the oldest. The most magnificent cities of all. We can't afford to lose a single one of them to him."

"Don't you have soldiers of your own in your cities?"

"No."

"Why not? It makes sense," I struggled for a moment. "Instead of constantly having to kick Darrell out...to have a section of the army posted and ready. That way it's harder for him to get in, and even if there's a delay....you have a better chance of keeping him out." It took a lot out of me to say all that; I didn't even know if any of it made sense. My head was swimming. I started to gasp, and the fire in my lungs flickered back to life. He furrowed his brow, but I wouldn't let him shut me up. And I enjoyed his reaction too much.

He hadn't thought of that, that much I could see.

"That's a good idea. But"—

"But you said you had a large army....They can handle it. If one city is attacked, call in the guard from a neighboring one if you have to."

"Hmm." Erik stared out the window, pensive. I sighed and pushed my hands underneath my pillow. All this talking was making me exhausted.

When Erik looked at me, his blue eyes were bright though with hope or excitement I didn't know which. "I'll go speak to Mia about it. We can't spare many, with the problem at Auyen, but I think we could send out a few thousand around the kingdom to keep an eye on things." He stood quickly, eager to get the job done. The doctor came bustling out of the back room. I had the sudden suspicion he'd been eavesdropping.

"Leaving so soon, Your Majesty?'

Erik nodded. "She's getting tired."

"Oh." There was a short pause. "Well, don't worry. I shall take care of her." Aryan sounded as though he considered it a great responsibility. Something to put him in the king's graces, no doubt.

Erik looked down at me. "Listen to Aryan, all right. We need you to get well."

I nodded and rolled my eyes. "Sure, Your Highness. Whatever you say."

After he was gone, Aryan gave me a funny look. "What?"

He dropped his eyes, instantly turning red. "Nothing, nothing." He cleared his throat. He grabbed up his papers, gave me one more uncertain glance, and sauntered quickly out of the room.

Aryan didn't come back. I stared at the wall numbly, wishing I could get up out of this stupid bed and actually do something. I must have fallen asleep, because the next thing I knew, I was having a nightmare.

I AM STUCK BEHIND BARS, in a tiny cage with the others—fairies whose faces I can't put names to. Erik is gone. Aryan is gone. I lean against the hard, cold metal; I feel like I'm going to scream. They are all pleading to be released, and so am I.

Only I know no one will listen; warm tears roll down my cheeks, even as I join in their plea.

There is a large campfire to the left of us, with soldiers sitting around it. They are eating, ignoring us as though we aren't even there. And then one of them stands up and comes towards us.

It's Darrell. I want to scream again at the laughter that animates his eyes. He has no right to be here. He doesn't seem to hear what we're saying. What we're begging him for. He reaches through the bars and touches my face.

"The war will be won easily now...."

I AWOKE WITH A START, gasping. My body ached. I rolled over; the room was dim, I listened for the tell-tale sound of Aryan's footsteps.

I lay there, waiting for the nightmare to fade away. My heart rate dropped, and I rubbed my eyes sleepily. I almost fell asleep again.

I inched my way up into a sitting position and listened some more. When I heard nothing, I sighed, and flung the blanket aside. I slipped out and—oh, how wonderful it felt—walked to the door. My lungs and sides ached, but that was nothing compared to the fact that I was actually moving on my two feet again.

Opening the door slowly, I poked my head through the opening. The hallway was dark, too.

Yes! I heard the little voice in my head exclaim joyfully. I stepped out the door and shut it quietly behind me. Tiptoeing was easy on the deep, soft carpet. I couldn't make a sound, even if I'd wanted to. I stole down the corridor quickly. I passed door after door but, because I wasn't sure what they opened up to, I didn't try to go in. The last thing I wanted to do now was walk into his throne room or something. At the end of the hall, I stopped.

I looked around, trying to decide what to do. There were two large doors on either side of me, and I didn't know which one to take. I reached for the one at my right, hesitated, stopped, bit my lip. I looked at the other one, considered. In the end I chose the right, turning the old handle slowly and pushing it open.

Darkness blinded me for a minute, but once my eyes adjusted, the light of the moon was enough for me to see that I was in a very big, round room with a gothic-type ceiling. I saw the dark images of furniture in front of me. I reached, feeling along the wall for a light. It occurred to me that maybe they didn't have lights here. My heart sunk. How was I going to explore without a light?

I stumbled along, into the room. I felt around everywhere for something to turn on.

My hand knocked something over, I caught it before it hit the floor and sighed with relief. I put it back and hunted until I found the lamp.

Of course, it didn't have a button, or a switch, or anything like that. I turned it over, and even took it to the window to have a better look at it as I searched for a way to turn it on. It didn't even have a light bulb. I moved my hands over its surface, completely confused.

Then the light flickered. I stopped, and it went out. I ran my hand over the surface again, the light flickered, and stayed. I smiled.

I couldn't see where the light was coming from, it was like it was being radiated from the lamp itself. I set it down on the table carefully and turned to face the room.

All along the curving walls were bookshelves that ran up to the very ceiling. I moved closer and touched one. It felt old, fragile. Its covers were old and faded, curling at the edges. I wondered what it was about. I pulled it out gently......

A brighter light flicked on. A fairy was standing in the doorway, arms crossed, fury plain on his features. "What do you think you're doing here?"

Uh-oh. I held up the book.

"You're not supposed to be here," he told me.

I made a face. Erik had showed up behind him. "Daniel."

The dark-haired fairy jumped a little, and turned to him; he bowed gracefully. "Your Majesty. I was just about to take her," he flashed a look at me. "Out." I dropped my eyes and wondered if 'out' was the fairy term for prison.

Serious blue eyes glared at my face. "Bethany, why aren't you in your room?"

"I'm bored."

"You're also stubborn. Not to worry, Daniel. She's fine."

"Your Majesty?"

"She has the authority to go wherever she pleases...once she recovers." His eyes looked at me pointedly.

"I am recovered, thank you."

He shook his head. "Women."

"Fairy kings."

He struggled not to smile. "What did you find?" He reached his hand out for the book, and I handed it to him. "You may go now, Daniel," he said without looking up from the book.

Daniel bowed again, keeping his eyes on me, and left. I noticed he glanced over his shoulder a couple of times.

Erik was looking through the book.

"Who told you I was gone?"

"Aryan noticed your cot was empty," he muttered.

Of course. "I didn't think he'd be back."

He laughed. "He's an odd one, it's true." Erik snapped the book shut, then and handed it to me. "Good choice. Though I don't think I've ever read that one before." He went over to the shelves and withdrew a beaten-up red book, which he handed to me. "This is too; you might find what you learn in them useful later on." He smiled at me, then, and I suddenly wondered just what kind of work it was I had to be doing here.

But I grinned back at him. "Thank you."

"Well, I wouldn't want for you to be bored."

I rolled my eyes. "You would be too if all you were allowed to do all day was sleep and stare at a wall."

"Trust me, before this is over, you'll *wish* that's all you had to do is sit and stare at a wall."

"I really doubt that."

"You will."

"Don't think so."

We were walking back up the hall now; the lights were still off and I stumbled over a short step on the way through. How had I missed that?

Erik didn't rush me as we sauntered along. He didn't seem to have a care in the world, as he walked beside me, hands clasped behind his back, talking. I wanted to ask him about the Auyen city, and what was happening there, but I remembered my nightmare and changed my mind. I'd ask later.

Aryan was sitting behind a tall white desk, he looked up as we arrived.

"There you are! Where did you get off to?" He stood and bowed. "Beg pardon, Your Majesty, it won't happen again."

Erik grinned. "Don't worry so much, doctor. It's not like she walked off the cliff or anything. She's fine."

Aryan looked at the books I held. "You took her to the hall of records?"

"No. She found it on her own."

I blushed, realizing then why Daniel had been so furious when he found me there. He probably thought I was a spy. I shuffled over to my bed and sat down, placing the books beside me.

"When will you be over?"

"Tomorrow morning before breakfast, probably. I will have a lot to do then."

"How's things in the city?"

His face fell. "Fine. I don't think he can hold out much longer, the way we have it surrounded."

"But?"

"But something's wrong. We haven't been able to tell for sure, but we think he's using the Auyen as a diversion for something else."

"Like what?"

"That's the problem. We don't know." He exhaled.

Aryan was listening to our conversation sadly, his forehead creasing deeply. I couldn't think of anything to say. "Of course it could just be we're getting paranoid," Erik continued. "Darrell is so sly, sometimes we expect a surprise move when there is none."

"That's not necessarily a bad thing."

Aryan's eyes flashed to my face.

"No? It makes for a lot of anxiety. A lot of panic among my people. Tomorrow morning I have a meeting planned with the generals to figure out just how to handle this issue from now on."

"Are you sending soldiers to the other cities?"

He smiled. "Yes. You should have been there when I told them about our conversation. Mia's ashamed she didn't think of it herself."

"Advisors aren't always right."

"I suppose not." Erik's short laugh was bleak.

"Your Majesty, might I talk to you?" Aryan said suddenly, looking for the world like he was about to faint.

"Certainly." Erik waved a hand to the door. As Aryan passed, he gazed at me. "Good night, Bethany."

"Good night, Erik. Don't let the issues keep you awake."

He chuckled dryly. "I'll try."

After they were gone, I leaned back and picked up the faded yellow book. It was heavy. When I opened it, I saw it was written in golden, odd-shaped runes. I frowned. How was I supposed to understand this?

I dropped it on the bed beside me and picked up the red one. This too, had been written in runes. I groaned.

CHAPTER NINE

Unbelievable. Why didn't Erik say anything to me about this? I pouted. Maybe, like everything else in this world, things worked differently than it did in mine. Maybe, if I rubbed my hand over the page as I had with the lamp....I gave it a try.

It didn't work.

Frustrated, I turned it over and tried to decipher the code on the back of the book, I shook it. Nothing happened.

I threw it to the floor. It was just as well that I couldn't read it, I hadn't wanted to anyway.

A soft golden light enveloped the book when it hit the floor. I watched, amazed, as the light faded away. I threw the other one. It landed, hitting the first squarely in the side. They both glowed brightly for an instant, then it stopped. I got up and bent over to pick them off the floor.

I opened the red book to the first page carefully, squinting so the light wouldn't blind me. But it didn't glow again. And to my surprise, I read and understood all the words easily. I shrugged, pleased with my ingenuity, and plopped back down on the bed for a read. It seemed to be a strange compilation of history, told in part, like a story. Only the names of many specific places were not included in the book. My brow furrowed.

On the third month of the year 290 of King Or's reign, his wife and their son, Darrell went to the city of S.__ where a board of delegates awaited their arrival. A horrible earthquake had ravaged the city, and the impoverished fae were in desperate need to rebuild. Or went there for the express purpose of aiding the fairies in the process in any way he and his family could.

The book went on to describe the various charity work which the royals took to during their stay at the city. I skipped a couple of pages. My eyes caught Darrell's name, and I stopped. *Prince* Darrell, I frowned at the thought the words implied.

It seemed he'd had no interest in the rebuilding plans and wanted more and more to separate himself from the family. It was even recorded that he spent three days completely absent. As far as I could tell, they had no idea where he had gone.

Lady Matilda was given a lot of credit for upholding the family's dignity and she stayed by her husband's side throughout the ordeal, though it was also noted she "spent many a night crying herself to sleep over her son", who at that time, was believed to be lost.

"Hmmm...." I mused to myself, suspicious.

Darrell wasn't lost. He'd come back in his own time, worse than before, resenting his mother's embraces and tears as much as his father's stern rebuke when Or found out that he'd left of his own will, and not that of another. The family left S_ in shatters.

There was a three-month time gap, in which nothing was said about anything apart from financial records of the empire, and several rumors that Darrell had run away to the human world.

I stopped reading there. Had he really? Did he really know my world? I scowled. If he did, it certainly didn't bode well for us humans. Who knew what kind of trouble he could have been causing?

On the next page was a copy of a letter, written to the king and queen to congratulate them on the day Erik was born. I read that part over, several times, amazed at what this graceful flowing hand had to say about the new prince.

From birth, it seemed, the kingdom put its faith in little Erik. Hopes resounded where there formally had been none. The delegate sent his strong wishes that Erik grow up handsome and true to the long line of kings that preceded him, and (I think this was meant seriously meant, though it was certainly jokingly written) that he might even teach Darrell a thing or two.

I chuckled at that and read on. There were no more natural disasters to talk about. The kingdom's money supply was good, nearly all fairies seemed to be living comfortably and happily, thanks to the good king Or.

The royal family went for an outing, several months after the birth of the new prince. The book never mentioned the name of the place, but it was said to be very beautiful, with crystal waters and glorious mountains rising above the soft green plains.

There was no mention of trouble this time.

I was on the lookout, however, tense. I certain something bad was going to happen amidst all that beauty and serenity.

There was a break in the story, where the author had apparently decided to include article about a new discovery by a fairy named Lykke. A long-time scientist and inventor, he'd finally accomplished the one thing he's committed his life to—and that was the capturing and safe use of light. I thought of the odd lamp in the hall of records and wondered if that had been his invention.

It said he'd produced something of an odd-shaped piece of glass, polished and shaped with rocks from the bottom of the L_ river. He had then opened up the glass, and placed into it a special mixture of chemicals, and the water from the Niger Sea, and sealed it back up again. Even behind the glass, the mixture was sensitive enough to light when met by any kind friction. Such as moving one's hands over the glass, for example.

Lykke said he hoped it was an invention that would prove useful for many years. And, I thought to myself, it had. I couldn't think of anything more ingenious. It was more amazing than the light bulb. No need to replace the light-giving substance, and the outside of the lamp was extremely durable.

That same year, a small band of fairies were taken to the dungeon for conspiracy. It was suspected Darrell had a part of inciting them against his father. Heavy emphasis on "suspected."

Or had defended his son's integrity, though the delegates and judges looked upon it as a sad, betrayed father protecting his son out of love. He was pitied, and the accusations ceased. The whole kingdom now worried over Or's safety for as long as Darrell abided in his home.

Meanwhile, Erik seemed to grow well in the eyes of the public. In the year 300 of his father's reign, he had already proved himself to be of an upright, and intelligent character. His mother, "who deigned to teach him herself," was proud to acknowledge that at the age of ten, he was already fluent in three out of the kingdoms twelve languages, and "far excelled her in the knowledge and application of mathematics." I smiled a little at that and read on. What charmed them the most was his obvious love for his parents and country.

Darrell's behavior had not gotten much better over the years, though he was no longer openly involved in crimes. His father and mother were taking extra steps to make sure Erik wasn't around him.

I was saddened by this fact. Poor Erik never really had the chance to get to know his brother. Even though I knew why, and because of that, knew the wisdom of the choice, I couldn't help but pity them both. I couldn't imagine what it would be like to not have Tracy to lean on every now and then.

Erik made his first trip alone when he was fifteen. Or was ill, and there had just been an enormous bout of rain in the East. Houses, businesses and schools had been either wiped out or devastated. As with any disaster, the royal family was expected to come to the aid of the destitute fairies. And so Erik went.

The long chapter detailed how Erik had gone confidently, to be faced by the crowds of homeless fairies and school-less teachers. He didn't seem ruffled or angered by them when some, in their grief, insulted his family in their anger. He only seemed very disturbed by the pain caused; he promised that he and his family would do anything they could to help.

A lot like a typical politician, I thought.

But Erik kept his word. He donated enough money to take care of the majority of the losses and left the fairies to take care of the rest. It seemed the royal family believed in keeping the citizens self-reliant. I had read that Or had done something similar to this when the earthquake had rocked S_.

I heard a sound and looked up. It was Aryan. He gave me a scolding look. "It's too early to be up."

"But—"

He took the book away and placed it on the stand beside my bed. "It'll still be here in the morning. Go to sleep."

I sighed heavily and slid down onto my back. He saw the frustration in my eyes. I didn't mention I'd never gone to bed in the first place; that would just get me into more trouble.

"Look at it this way—the more sleep you get, the more likely it is that you'll heal quickly."

I woke up early, just as one of the suns was starting to shine through my window. I sat up, rubbed my lamp gently, and picked up the book again.

Darrell and Erik fought hard in the 315th year—Erik had been twenty-five, and Darrell had been somewhere in his forties, both still very young by fairy standards. I doubted if Darrell looked much older than nineteen at the time, given his youthful appearance in the meadow.

Erik had caught Darrell stealing from Matilda's jewelry closet. His bag had been nearly overflowing with the jewels....Which was the last thing the family needed, and the breaking point for Erik. Trouble had been brewing between the boys ever since Erik found out Darrell's support of the fairy gang back in the nineties. He wanted Darrell thrown out of the palace, making it clear to everyone he perceived his brother as a threat to the family. He didn't trust him, and the fact that he'd never spent a full day with him in his life obviously contributed to that fact.

Matilda was once again torn, grieved that her oldest son would drag her family through so many scandals, and heartbroken at the same time of that blatant dislike he showed both for her and his father. She heeded Erik's pleas and forced Darrell to leave the palace.

Or's input was not included in this section of history, there was no mention of him, and I supposed that something particularly nasty had occurred that hadn't been reported. I didn't believe Darrell would leave peacefully under any circumstances.

It was suspected—again with the "suspected"—that Darrell had tried to get back into his parents' favor. For a while, his act seemed genuine. But just before they welcomed him back, it had been found out that he'd fallen in love with a woman whom the King and Queen did not approve. A gypsy woman. They fought again. And Darrell refused to give her up.

He was not written of again for a space of about fifty years. When he was, it was only to mention again that he had been seen coming in and out of the human world.

Towards the end of Or's reign, Darrell showed up once again to take up the throne. The dying Or made it perfectly clear to him, that he wanted nothing to do with him who had tried so often to undermine him, and had shown his mother no love since the day he was born. Instead, according to Matilda's wishes, Erik was to inherit the kingdom and everything that went along with it.

The fairy had been so infuriated by the news as to cause a scene in the sick chamber, demanding what he called his rights as the firstborn, accusing his father of breaking the tradition.

But Or was strong. He neither compromised nor tried to reason with his son. He'd chosen the path to take, and he was going to take it.

He did have one last comment to make, however, and that was that it was perfectly fine to break a tradition in choosing the younger son over the older, if all elder had to offer his people was death.

I read that last paragraph three times, trying to soak it all in. I'd certainly gotten myself into a ton of trouble by agreeing to come here.

Erik came in then, and I set the book down. "Finally, a real live person."

"Quit complaining." But he laughed. He noticed the book in my hand. "Done already?"

"It was interesting."

He rolled his eyes.

"Looking forward to the meeting?" I asked sarcastically.

"Not really. Basically that's all I'm going to hear about is how impossible everything is going to be."

"Sounds like you need some new generals."

"They need to be motivated. Stripping them of their titles won't do me any good. We haven't had a war here in thousands of years. The old way of doing things is outdated; we have weapons, cities we didn't have before. Complications...." Erik rubbed his face wearily. "We're going to have to come up with a new way of dealing with him entirely. Which is going to be hard since he's spent so much time in your world observing your wars and battles. He knows things my men don't."

I thought about that for a minute. There was a possibility Darrell brought back more from my world than just knowledge, but I wasn't sure how to tell Erik that. "What are you going to suggest?"

"I'm going to tell them that as far as the Auyen city goes, we have to get the prisoners out—that's our first priority. We'll send a few spies in to scout it out and find where they are. If possible, we'll get them out without a battle, I'd hate to see that city go but we may not have a choice. But if we can sneak the hostages out, we can hunker down and wait him out. There's not much food in the city now. He won't be able to stick it out for more than a few weeks."

"Hm," I nodded. "And I suppose you have a date set for that." It wasn't a question.

"That depends," he looked at me. "I suppose you want a hand in it."

"I do. But I might not get well enough in time."

"You will. We'll be getting our men together and sending in the spies later tonight, if all goes well. You should be fine by the time they come to report the fairies whereabouts."

I nodded. Then a thought suddenly crossed my mind. "Where's Aryan?"

"Tending to another of his patients. He's uneasy...." Erik trailed off, gazing out the window.

"About me," I finished and he looked me in the face.

"Yes."

"Because I'm human."

Erik hesitated. His expression grew dark. "Yes," he said finally, looking away from me. I took a deep breath. It seared my lungs; I winced, glad now that he wasn't looking at me. I tried to continue.

"And Darrell has been among my people."

Erik flinched. "Yes."

I nodded. "...And, I got into the hall of records last night."

"Of course, he thinks you're working with Darrell."

"Can't you tell him I'm not? You know, before he decides I'm too dangerous to keep around or something?" I glanced at the vials on the shelf across the room. Erik paled.

"He wouldn't dare. He knows that'd be one very quick way to obtain an execution."

"Maybe so, but I don't necessarily favor the possibility. The way he looks at me...."

"Ignore it. There is no possibility."

"Don't be naïve." I paused. "I'm going to guess that's what he wanted to talk to you about last night." Erik nodded, and I blinked.

"This isn't going to be easy."

A small smile tugged at his lips. "I'm surprised you thought it would be."

"I didn't. But I also didn't think there was such a thing as fairy racism."

Erik laughed at me, then. I wrinkled my nose at him and turned to the window, muttering to myself.

"Fairy racism," he mocked, still laughing.

"Well, it's true. How else would you describe it?"

"Paranoia," he chortled.

A young redhead walked in carrying a tray filled with some wonderful smelling pastries. Erik stood up.

"Tell me how it goes."

"I will."

I gaped at the tray she set before me; the sheer amount made my stomach hurt. I struggled my way through half the plate, to be polite.

"It's nice to see you're eating," she commented, obviously pleased.

I smiled and picked up the other book to kill some more time. The sun was high in the sky, I heard some strange bird singing in the bushes by my window, though I couldn't see it. It was a magnificent sound; soothing, lilting tones flowed through the air, carried by the soft breeze to my ears. I leaned back against the pillows contently, flipping the pages.

This book was different. Unlike the strange history book, this was composed of poems, dreamed up by fairies long before I was born. Or Erik was born, probably.

I was about a quarter of the way through the book when he came back. By the look on his face, I could tell things had gone well. Good. We were moving forward, at least.

He stopped by my bed, his hands in his pockets. "We'll send them out tonight. With any luck they should be back in a couple of weeks."

"And I'll be out of here by then, right?"

"Yes, you should be." His eyes sparkled; he looked around. "Where's Aryan? Hasn't he been in this morning?"

I shook my head. "No."

"Hm." Erik's face went rigid. "I'll be back." He stormed out the door. I turned back to the poetry.

Erik came back a few minutes later with Aryan. I could hear him speaking harshly, angrily. Aryan's quiet excuses seemed only to make him angrier.

"I don't care if you have half the kingdom to care for! You take care of Bethany first, before *anyone* else."

Aryan stuttered something I couldn't hear.

"That doesn't matter. You can't just desert her here for hours at a time without checking up on her, what if something happens?"

Which it won't. I rolled my eyes. He was such a worrier. That's one thing I'd learned about him so far.

Aryan mumbled.

"I don't care," Erik snapped.

He came in, then, followed by a humbled Aryan who hurried to get my medicine and give it to me while Erik eyeballed him. I gave him a look like, see what I meant about him, and took the medicine.

I shoved the poems to the side and sat up straighter, eyeing Erik. "What?"

"I want to go for a walk."

He looked at Aryan, who waved his hand and exhaled dismissively. "Just don't take too long, Bethany. I don't want you to get exhausted."

I nodded and stood.

"She can't very well go out looking like that," someone said. A woman with long shiny obsidian hair and dark eyes stood in the threshold, looking me carefully.

"Ah. Mia," Erik greeted her. "You haven't met Bethany yet, have you?"

"No." She nodded in my direction. I smiled.

"Hi."

Mia was small for a fairy. She was about my height, and thin. She motioned to the hallway. "Let's get you fixed up first."

"It's not like she's going to the courthouse, Mia," Aryan objected. "She won't be gone for more than an hour or so."

She snapped around towards him, eyes flashing. Apparently I wasn't not the only one he irked.

"Are you a woman?"

"No."

"Then I doubt you would understand." She looked back to me. "Come with me, Bethany." I followed her down the sunlit hallway to a large room just around the corner. "It'll do you some good to get away from that old flea bag, anyway," she grumbled.

"Actually, he's been avoiding me."

She gave me a funny look. "He's a queer fairy. I wouldn't trust him."

"I have to admit, I've been keeping an eye on which vials he gives me medicine from."

Mia laughed. She opened a creamy colored door and stepped to a brightly decorated room. There was a long mirror on the south wall, directly across from the door.

It wasn't until then that I realized what a mess I really was. My hair was knotted and dirty; I had a mark on my cheek from the collapse I'd had out in the woods, and I was still in the clothes I'd worn on Thursday. I didn't even know what today was. Mia had been right.

She called in a couple of maids and helped wash my hair; they told me to go take a bath while they fished out some clothes that would fit me.

They found me a long pink dress with a fitted waist and a long slash of white down the side. I dressed quickly, thinking I could throw my hair up into a ponytail and be out the door, but they wouldn't let me go that easily. They made me sit down while they braided it and Mia even had the insistence to shove a tiny blue flower into my hair.

I had to admit, I looked pretty darn cute when they were done with me. I hugged Mia and thanked her.

"I just couldn't see the sense in letting you out like that," she told me, smiling, tugging at the hem of her uniform a bit. It shocked me to remember that this woman was a general. She seemed so much more like a royal herself.

I found Erik waiting for me in the hall. He smiled at me when I bounded through the door.

Before we could go anywhere, Daniel came into sight. "Your Majesty," he murmured, bowing. Daniel shot a glare at me.

Erik inclined his head. "What is it, Daniel?"

"Nothing sir, I only wanted to know how the girl was fairing."

"Ask her yourself."

Daniel looked at me. "She doesn't look sick," he said skeptically. I stiffened, sensing an accusation in his tone. Erik took my wrist and pulled me away from Daniel, towards the door.

"I don't like what you are implying."

"I only meant that you were looking better, my lady."

I snorted. "Fairy racism."

"Sorry." Erik seemed abashed, he put a hand against my back to push me gently away.

"You're not the one doing it, it's him and that other one—even Mia thinks he's insane."

"Unfortunately, he's the only doctor for hundreds of miles. Fairies don't get sick often."

"Hmm." I sulked.

Erik guided me to the door and opened it for me. I stepped out into the fresh morning air. The trees and sky seemed especially bright today. Maybe that's because I'd been in the sick room for so long. I didn't know. All I knew was that it felt wonderful to be outside again.

I felt a crazy impulse to go to my favorite waterfall. My heart sunk when I remembered I was no longer a part of that world. That there was a chance I never would be again. I took a deep breath to distract myself and looked at Erik.

"Where to?"

He pointed the way. I saw a few fairies, dressed in bright summer gowns like I was, with baskets full of freshly cut flowers or apples. I waved at them happily. Erik observed my actions with bright eyes.

We were nearing a little white gazebo. The sun was setting the water on fire with sparkling beams of light. I wished I could look at it longer, it was so delicious, but I had to turn my eyes away for it was too bright. I gazed towards the forest; somehow that great mysterious thing never seemed to be far from us here.

"Happy now?"

"Very." I grinned up at him, and he smiled back.

"Good. I've been wondering, how you've been getting along. Whether you've begun to think maybe...you shouldn't have come."

I was quiet for a moment. "At first, I did think it was a mistake. I'm not usually that impulsive," I laughed at myself. "And I'm still not sure what you think I can do here for you. I'm nothing special at all." I looked away from his frown, towards the water again. "But the more I think about it.... It's amazing to be here. I never dreamed of a place so beautiful in my whole life." I shook my head; I didn't have the words to describe it all. I looked up at him, hoping he understood.

He seemed to.

I nudged his arm playfully. "And, you know, you're pretty cool too." I chuckled.

"Well, that's a relief. The way you acted yesterday"—

"Yesterday I was in lockup. I had a right to be grumpy."

Erik raised his eyebrows.

By this time we'd reached the gazebo, I sat down on its silky soft bench immediately. I wouldn't tell him, but I was starting to get a little tired. And I didn't want to go back yet. I watched the women working in the garden. They must very strong to carry such large baskets, full of fruit, and still keep one arm free to pick more. I shook my head, wondering if I would ever be so strong. Strong enough to save them from Darrell's army.

"I needed an escape from my old world anyway, I guess."

"Hmm." He was watching the water. "Why?"

"You didn't notice? Marissa and Tanya are hanging out more than usual. Something's wrong."

"I wasn't aware that it was a crime to 'hang out' with someone, as you call it."

"That's not it, really. I don't even know *what* it is, but I can feel it. There's something going on that I don't know about and it bothers me. It makes me worry...."

"Didn't you ask her about it?"

"About what?" I rolled my eyes. "Hey, Marissa, how come you weren't in school when you were supposed to be sick? That doesn't make any sense."

"You don't believe she was sick, though. What if she's in trouble?"

I didn't say anything. He repeated his question.

"If she is, she should have told me. She knows I'll help her through anything, I always have, so there's no reason why I wouldn't now. But if I went up to her and told her to her face I think she lied to the school, she'd bite my head off and I really don't need that right now." I looked down, playing with the sequins on my dress. "She's just acting weird, that's all. They both are. I don't understand it."

Erik was quiet; he was looking off into the distance, a thoughtful expression on his face.

Someone shouted, a little boy was running across the grassy lawn, towards one of the working women. He grabbed onto her leg and said something to her in a demanding tone, hopping up and down as he did so.

She reached lithely into her basket and drew out a large, red fruit which she promptly handed to him. He took the food and ran off, holding it high for the other boys to envy. I chuckled quietly.

Just then I saw Aryan come stalking around the corner. I hopped up.

"C'mon, I want to walk over by the water." Away from the doctor.

I tweaked his arm as I passed by, pulling him out of his thoughts. Erik got up silently and followed me.

I snuck a glance over my shoulder. Aryan didn't appear to have seen us yet. But he was definitely looking. I would have asked to take a walk in the woods, but I thought that might give me away. Erik hadn't noticed my intentions yet, still wrapped up in his thoughts. I tweaked his arm again.

"What?"

"Nothing, just thinking." He couldn't have picked a more frustrating answer. We walked along the sparkling water, till we reached a spot where the river curved. The mountains rose out of the ground, miles away. They looked so close here, so *huge*. I blinked and started towards them. I wasn't about to let Aryan catch me just yet. I wasn't done exploring. My lungs ached mildly, nothing compared to the excruciating pain before.

Erik followed more slowly now, I sensed he was thinking about turning back. I added a little hop to my step and hurried along so he'd have to hurry too.

Of course, I forgot about the whole super-speed thing.

He caught my arm. "Come on, Bethany. Time to head back."

I huffed and turned around obediently. Maybe if I was good, Aryan would let me out again before sunset.

His fat fumbling form appeared in the distance, headed in the opposite direction. The children were sprinting towards us, yelling and laughing with each other. It was impossible not to catch some of their joy. It was contagious.

One little boy made it to us first. He stopped and bowed, but, to my surprise, he didn't bow to his king; he bowed to me.

"Your highness."

I giggled. "Why hello, what's your name?"

"Nate." As he looked up at me, some of his pale blond hair fell into his eyes he pouted and shoved it out of the way.

The other kids skidded and tumbled beside him. They were so full of energy, I wished I felt the same. They all bowed to both me and Erik. One small girl even asked me how I was feeling. I glanced at Erik, surprised, but he just shrugged.

"Everyone knows."

"Ah." I wasn't sure I liked that idea. "I'm fine," I told the little girl. "I feel much, much better now." I picked her up and we all went back to the palace together. Aryan stopped us.

"There you are! I thought I said one hour."

"A few extra minutes won't kill her, Aryan," Erik told him in an authoritative voice. Aryan's shoulders hunched at bit at his tone. I set the little fairy girl on the ground. She instantly whipped around and grabbed Erik's hand. He smiled down at her.

"Won't your mama be worried, little one?"

"Uh-oh!" And she was off, running to find her mother. We snickered and followed the panting Doctor Aryan back to the sick room.

A pang of dread hit me as I stepped back into the room. I hated it here; I hadn't realized I'd stopped until Erik put his hand on my shoulder to guide me in.

"Just a couple more days," he reminded me.

I marched over to my cot and sat down on the edge, more grateful for that soft little bed than I wanted to be. I awoke a few hours later, feeling a jolt and hoping it wasn't nighttime yet. I sat up and turned quickly for the window. The sun was going down, no doubt, but it was nowhere near twilight yet. That was good.

Aryan was staring at me from behind his desk.

"Nightmare?"

"Nearly." He frowned, but I didn't bother to explain.

I ran my hand through my hair. My fingers caught on the flower Mia had put there and pulled it out. It was dead, but still strikingly blue. It was amazing how bright the colors were here. I set the flower down on the table carefully.

Aryan surprised me by handing me a book. "I have to check on a few patients. I'll be back soon." It sounded like he wanted me to relay the message in case Erik got here and he hadn't returned yet. I smiled at him.

"Okay." I watched him go, amused. The book was a difficult book to read, as much as I enjoyed it. The fairy terms were all new to me, and I found myself learning as I read.

The days passed quickly; every day I was a little better. My walks with Erik grew longer, and more frequent. I could see Aryan was pleased to see me recover so fast, probably because it meant I would be out of his hair soon.

Finally, one morning Aryan told me I should be able to leave the sick room soon. Tomorrow, maybe. He handed me a brand-new book, and suggested I use it to pass the time while he went to check up on some other patients.

It was a little book of poems. Minutes flew by as I read the fluent, musical lines, envisioning the bright scenes and heavy emotions they implied. Sorrow, grief, regret, joy, love, jealousy....all had been somehow incorporated into one poem. I was amazed at how easily I could understand it, just weeks ago I hadn't had clue one about faerie literature. I read the book over twice, trying to memorize it, then set it down. I got up and opened the window.

The air smelt of honeysuckle and strawberries. I breathed it in hungrily. Never in my life had I imagined a place like this. It didn't seem real. My eyes opened again and I stuck my head out the window.

Calls resonated through the gardens, mothers and fathers calling out to their children, telling them it was time for dinner, time to leave, to nap.....As I shut the window, I heard other voices. The first was Daniel's, but the second I couldn't recognize.

"What are we going to do about her?"

"I don't know. The king seems to think she's worth something to us."

"I don't think so. The sooner we get rid of her the better."

My heart skipped a beat.

Daniel spoke up. "I don't think so. I think we should wait."

"For what." The fairy's voice was dead.

"What if he's right?"

"So what if he is? She's *human*, Daniel, she doesn't belong with us. I want her gone."

There was a long silence.

Erik came in. He was smiling, but when he saw my pale, horrified face, his happy expression disappeared.

"What's wrong?"

I shook my head. "Did you see Daniel in the hallway?"

"Yes"—

"Who was that with him?"

"I didn't see anyone with him, Bethany. Why what's wrong?"

"I just heard someone tell him to kill me."

CHAPTER TEN

Erik was sitting with me on the cot. He'd called the guards to search the grounds for Daniel and the man that had been with him.

They'd been searching for two hours.

I had the feeling Erik wanted to be out there as well, to throttle them both when he found them, but he was afraid to leave me alone.

Mia was there, standing in the corner by the threshold, hands behind her back, eyes staring blindly ahead. She hadn't moved since she got here.

"We should send her out; she can prove herself that way, it's the only way anyone will ever believe she's really on our side."

"She doesn't need to prove anything." Erik snapped.

Mia didn't respond to that, but her body language made it clear that she did not agree.

I didn't see any way out of it. No matter what happened, people—fairies—weren't going to want me around. There was nothing anyone could do about it, I might as well face up and get the job done as quickly as possible so I could go home.

Aryan had found his way back, and was fidgeting behind his desk. "It's going to be fine, they'll find them."

"Of course they will." But I doubted it.

A guard ran in, gun in hand. "We lost them, Your Majesty. Daniel's chamber has been cleared out. There's no way to tell where he went."

Erik's face fell. "Keep searching. I want them found. Those two could be the end of us if they walk free."

The guard bowed low and went off the way he had come. Slowly, I got up.

"Bethany?"

"I have to do something. I can't just sit here and wonder what's going to happen."

But Erik just looked at me with cheerless eyes. He didn't say anything.

I turned to Aryan.

"Am I well enough to work?"

He nodded slowly, rubbing his chin. "So long as you take it slow, dearie." That "dearie" sounded clumsy on his lips, but I ignored it.

"Then I want to start now." Erik was about to object, but I cut him off. "We might as well get some work done without sitting around feeling sorry for ourselves. Any suggestions, Mia?"

Mia thought for a moment. "I think we could use you in the strategic sector, now that you mention it. Our people don't really know how to handle war anymore." She smiled halfheartedly.

"Fine, then." I moseyed past Erik. "Coming or not?"

I saw him get up out of the corner of my eye. He led me out of the sickroom into a different, heavily carpeted hallway. Pictures lined the walls on either side of us. I guessed they were members of the royal family though none of the fairies in them seemed to bear any distinction: they were dressed plainly, in gowns and suits I'd seen other fairies wear. Grim expressions marked every visage I passed, however, and I felt a shiver flow down my spine. I was suddenly unsure that Daniel was the only fairy I was going to have to worry about.

Erik was silent as he led me down the hallway. I wished that I could say something to reassure him, but no words came. I played with a lock of my hair uncomfortably. Thinking.

At the end of the hall, beneath a giant sparkling chandelier, Erik opened a door for me and stood aside silently. Mia walked in beside me. She cleared her throat, and everyone turned towards us, suddenly silenced. I noticed many of them wore the same dark blue uniform as Mia and wondered if that meant they were all generals.

My body tensed. How was I going to do this?

Mia introduced me calmly, telling them all why I was there and what had just happened. She asked them all to listen without prejudice. "I can assure you, she is not with Darrell," she ended, a stiff smile on her face. "He tried to kidnap her not too long ago, I hear. And she fought them off rather well."

There were many hushed murmurs at this. Three dozen eyes appraised me with approval...or disbelief. I somehow found the courage to smile at them. My head swam; Mia's hand suddenly was on my elbow, holding me up.

She took me to the head of the long table and sat down beside me. I braced myself, not knowing quite what to do yet. And Mia, seeing my discomfort, broke the ice for us all with a question I think most of them had on their minds about that time.

"As you no doubt have heard, Darrell has spent a lot of time in your world, watching how your people do things...." She trailed off. "What did he bring back?"

I told her that, not being part of his plan, I didn't know exactly what he'd brought back, but that it was most likely he'd stolen some secrets from various armies around the globe, and had obtained by now an in depth perception of the art of warfare. He probably had some weapons, too.

I stressed that last part, knowing that they hadn't considered that possibility at all, just by looking at their shocked faces. I reminded them to divide up parts of the army and put them in various cities of the empire—giving more to the most vulnerable ones.

I also told them that it would be a good idea to send several spies to 'enlist' in his army, to find out just what he was doing. That way we could more easily trump his efforts.

"Another thing we could do is sabotage his system. Take away from him the weapons he has and turn them against him."

"But how do we do that?"

"Use your spies. They're discreet, are they not?"

They were silent.

Another young fairy came burst in the door. He stood before us, panting. "They're back."

"What?" I heard fairies demand. Something had gone wrong, my heart lurched at the sight of the young fairy's fierce expression.

"They were turned back at the borders. Darrell's army wouldn't even hear of them walking through it."

My eyes narrowed. "Try again."

"But, Lady, His"—

"I don't care what His Majesty decreed, I told you to try again."

"We won't get through!" He cried, frustrated.

"Yes, you will."

"How do you know?"

"Because...I'm going with you."

I got up. Mia was ahead of me, gliding through the open door.

"Tell the men," I pressed, gliding past him. I heard him heave a sigh behind me.

I met Mia in her room. She'd already picked out some dark clothes for me to wear. They were made of dark brown leather. "They won't get in your way," she told me, tying the back of the suit behind me. When she was done, she handed me a pair of tiny black shoes.

There was a loud knocking at the door. I slid the first shoe on, transferred the other into my right hand, and looked at her sideways. "That'd be him."

She opened that door just as I was pulling my hair up into a ponytail. Erik stalked inside.

"Where is she?"

"Right here." I fastened the rubber band into place and glanced at myself in the mirror. Not bad.

Erik's face was red. "Do you have any idea what you're doing?"

"Yup. I'm going to get them inside that city."

"You're insane."

"Erik, you said yourself Darrell doesn't have enough food to last a month. If anyone's going to pay for that, it'll be the prisoners. They'll die if we can't get them out."

"You won't get in. He's suspicious of everyone. And he's seen you before, remember."

"I do. I also have a plan."

"What's that?" he asked. I didn't like the way he seemed predisposed to brush off anything that came out of my mouth.

"I don't have enough time to tell you, Erik, I have to get going. You just take care of things here and I'll be back soon. Promise."

I picked up the tiny black weapon Mia had gotten out for me and headed for the door. He blocked my way. "Erik, come on."

Though he made no move to reply, his eyes darkened in response to my plea.

"I thought this was why I came here. What, you're going to tell me that all that time I spent in a sick bed was a waste of time?"

"Bethany..."

"Erik, *this* is what you went into my world for. To find someone to help. I'm here now and I'm going to help, whether you like it or not. If you didn't want me involved, you never should have asked me in the first place!"

"It's not that I don't want you to, Bethany, I'm just thinking about you, that's all."

He was enormously confused; I sighed. "Look, everything's going to be fine. Okay? I'll handle it. Give me four days, if I'm not back by then you can blast your way through the city if you want. Just give me a chance. I need to boost my approval rating anyway."

Erik glowered at that but stepped to the side. I pushed by him and Mia fell into step beside me; she filled me in with the general make-up of the Auyen city. At the doorstep I found twenty or so fairies in uniform, waiting for me, the frustrated guard and a general among them.

"Why's he coming?" I hissed to Mia.

"He wants to see how you do," she whispered back, and my stomach turned. Great. First Erik, now a babysitter. What next?

We made good time that night, making it to Auyen City—one of the four ancient Auyen cities, as I learned from General Leo—before midnight. We stopped outside, in the encampment where our men were waiting. They met us anxiously, casting uncertain glances in my direction, and turning to Leo for instruction.

He only stepped back, allowing me take charge. I wielded the sharp weapon in my hand, staring at the smoldering city. I felt a pang of sorrow as my eyes took in the hellish scene before me. Screams echoed in the distance, and then were abruptly cut off. The throbbing in my chest reappeared for the first time in weeks.

Doubt settled in. Would my plan work? What if it didn't? The screams that emanated from the village seemed to answer the second question, and I felt a tremor of fear.

I winced, turning to face the army. Their hopeless, fire-lit faces filled my heart with dread. I raised my head, trying to look more authoritative than I felt.

"You all need to pull out."

There was a gasp. They began to murmur, grimacing, glaring at me with accusing eyes. I ignored them, speaking only to the one I had to prove myself to now—Leo.

"Darrell is on guard for a reason. That reason is them"—I motioned to the soldiers with my arms—"the only way we'll be able to get in and out safely is if he doesn't expect us to do anything. Right now, he's expecting a battle. He won't open his gates for anything."

"But you said you'd get in."

"I'm not going through the gates; I'm going over the wall, and I'm taking you three with me." I pointed to the spies that'd tagged along. "Once we're over, we'll split up, find the prisoners and get them out. We'll send them up over the east wall, two at a time, if we can.

"I want men over there," I pointed. "In the tree line, watching for them. Once you see them start to go over, run over and help them, run them to the others quickly." I paused, staring at them hard. "I don't want any mistakes here, so you better not make any. I might just decide to leave you behind if you do."

"Is everyone clear on this?"

They nodded reluctantly, but I noticed that a few looked excited; particularly the spies.

"Does anyone have a *problem* with this?"

No one said a word. I nodded once, pursing my lips. "Then let's go."

"Make a show out of it," I added, as the men reached for their bags.

They got their things together loudly, took down their tents, and with many complaints against King Erik, they left. Once they were out of sight, I sat with the spies under the cover of a large tree. We waited. Several men shouted in the distance. One fairy hopped to his feet and started forward, but I planted a hand on his chest.

"Wait!" I huffed.

They weren't convinced. There was some commotion in the city, and then I heard the victorious cry of the army rise up in the air. I smiled and looked up. The moon was bright and immaculately white. I watched as a cloud sheathed its luminance, then arose from my crouch.

"Now!"

We slithered through the darkness to the high wall of the city's gates. It was old, with many cracks and crevices, and it was easy to climb over, though my lungs burned slightly, and my muscles felt like jelly by the time I got to the top. I thought briefly of Erik as I turned to climb down the other side. Maybe he'd been right after all.

The others were waiting for me at the bottom. One grabbed my waist and pulled me off the wall, setting me carefully on my feet.

We could hear the celebration going down in the center of town, it pleased me. The windows glowed yellow from the lights of the lamps, and I saw that many doors were open, spilling the light out into the stone street. An empty fruit cart stood beside the bar.

"Go!"

We took off in opposite directions. I went south, through the center of town. I tried to keep as much in the dark as I could, but it was hard when everyone's lights were on and the moon was uncovered again. I slunk behind the rows of old mansions and businesses, peeking in windows, investigating every sound. I had no idea what to look for here. The darkness reminded me of my nightmare, I shivered violently.

Then I approached a small stone house. This, unlike all the others, was dark. I crept up and looked through the window but didn't see anything. I went around to the door, checking over my shoulder to make sure no one was watching. I could feel the adrenaline coursing through my body, making it difficult to stay calm.

I pressed lightly on the door with my fingertips, and it swung open, groaning as the wood ground against the frame. I flinched and turned my head around. The streets were empty, excepting the one drunk fairy that was stumbling around near the corner, singing to himself.

Nevertheless, I stepped inside quickly. As soon as I was in, I was blind. I felt around, fearing what I would discover, only to be shocked that there was nothing in this little room. I ran my hand along the wall, until I found a doorknob. It wasn't locked, and I let myself in.

Almost immediately, my foot fell forward into nothingness, and my body shot downward. I rolled down the steep steps, desperately trying to reach out and grab *something*. My fingers found a crevice in the wall, and I gripped it, nearly ripping my arm out of the socket at the same time. My heart pounded, and my lungs burned. For two long seconds I sat there, panting, trying to relax. I wasn't going to get out of here alive if I panicked.

I slid off the step onto my feet and inched my way down. At the bottom of the stairs, I tripped on an overturned lamp. The dim light filled the tiny dank room. There was a table, and an empty shelf.

Nothing else. Frustration wrapped itself in a knot around my chest; I was nearly ready cry.

I was about to go when I noticed something. Jutting out of the wall, was a long piece of paper. I went over to it, set the lamp on the floor and gripped the block with both hands. I pulled it out gently and withdrew the paper.

Again, I couldn't read it, it was in runes. I shrugged and stuffed it in my pocket. Maybe Leo or Mia would know what it was. I shoved the block into place, turned out the light, and stumbled back up the stairs.

I continued my search, always thinking I'd found something, then always getting disappointed. Since I hadn't heard from any of my comrades, I decided they weren't doing any better. I refused to consider that they may have deserted me here.

Then, as I was investigating around an old deserted well, I saw something dark move out of the corner of my eye. I froze and turned slowly. But I didn't see it again. Carefully, I ambled over, weapon in hand, geared for a fight. I reached the corner, peeked around....

A young woman was huddled up in the corner, staring up at me with pleading eyes. I lowered the weapon, crouching down before her, looking over my shoulder again. She backed away quickly. Silently.

"Sshh!" I whispered before she could scream. "I'm here to help. Where are the others?"

She looked over her shoulder, into the dark cavern behind her. It looked like half of a building.

"Wait here." I got up, and whistled out a long, loud call, twisting and turning the notes so that they sounded like that of a bird. I held up one finger, showing her that she should wait yet still. She nodded jerkily and dropped her head onto her knees.

At the slightest sound, my body sunk into a defensive position, weapon already in hand; the pulse in my chest thudding along steadily with my heartbeat.

"Who's that?"

"Malcolm," someone hissed.

"Found them."

He was at my side instantaneously. I pointed to the house. "She says they're in there. You get them."

Malcom gave me a look, but the exhaustion was there, written on my face. He didn't argue. I stayed outside with the woman, watching for trouble. Within minutes Malcolm came out with a small band of fairies. We were leading them away when I spotted the other two spies across town, edging their way toward us. I felt a rush of satisfaction; this was going very well.

How long could it really last?

We reached the eastern wall; I showed the prisoners how to climb up the wall, waiting and pushing from behind those that were too slow. Soldiers materialized out of the darkness to lead them to the others in the forest.

The two spies had made it back, we didn't acknowledge each other, but I was relieved to see they'd made it safely through town. The party was dying down now, and soon it would be harder to get the prisoners through without being noticed.

I moved faster, carrying children over and pulling women over the barrier as quickly as I could.

Malcolm had with him the last group of prisoners. He was taking *forever*; I rushed over, and picked up one of the smallest ones and carried him on my hip through the town.

"Stop, stop!" someone hissed.

Everyone halted. Some frightened murmurs ran through the small group, but Malcolm and I quickly hushed them. A trio of fairies marched by us.

The night guard.

We huddled in the shadow of the house behind us as they past. They went down, past what looked like a schoolhouse, and turned a corner. We breathed a sigh of relief and started to move on.

"Ayyyyyaaaa....." squealed the baby. I quickly clapped a hand over his mouth, but it was already too late. They had heard. The crushing orb in my chest pounded as they ran towards us. I saw three others coming from across the street.

"Run!" I don't know who made the call, but I agreed with it. I handed off the little one to another woman. Malcolm grabbed my arm and raced me to the barrier.

It was pandemonium. Once they reached the wall they didn't know what to do. So they stayed put, standing there like fools. Malcolm raced up the wall with the baby, and only then did they begin the attempt. They climbed awkwardly, slipping down just when I thought they'd made it. I fought back the impatience.

"Hurry!" Leo called from the other side.

Shut up, Leo.

The others were closer now. A large hand grabbed my arm and spun me around.

Unhesitant, I introduced his face to my foot. He fell back, and I pushed another fairy to the wall.

"Climb!"

Why so slow! I wanted to throw them all over the wall.

They heard me but they were slow to react. I shoved four fairies towards it, and Malcolm called them up. He was helping a woman to the top and couldn't come down to help me.

My upper body hurt, and my head ached, but I couldn't stop. I had to protect them until it was safe for me to go up.

I felt the guard's arm coming before I actually saw it. Painfully, I twisted aside to avoid the blow. I sent my fist neatly into the hollow under his neck in return. He fell back with a choking sound.

A wrathful scream filled the air, I looked up, startled. It was him. He was running for us, weapon held high. The rest of his militia filed out behind him, carrying lanterns and torches.

I shot a look behind me. Half the fairies had gone over the wall. The rest were starting up it, pushing and shoving one another to get there.

You'll never get anywhere that way! I wanted to shout at them. But something hard hit me in the face. Blue fireworks erupted in front of my eyes; I felt my body falling. Then I began to panic; I could not be vulnerable. Not here.

When I opened my eyes, my face was in the dirt. A soldier was attacking the fairies at the wall. I lunged to my feet and ripped him away from them, grabbing the baby he'd taken hold of and shoving her back into her mother's arms. "Hurry!"

The fairy didn't move at first, shocked now that she could see my face in the light of the mob's torches.

I didn't have time to wait for her.

I turned on another rogue and kicked him in the solar plexus. My knees nearly gave out under me. I could feel my pulse beating in my brain. My limbs were shaking; I was painfully certain that only the energy of the orb in my chest was keeping me from collapsing again. What was I going to do if it stopped?

What had happened to Malcolm? The others?

"Come on!" Malcolm was suddenly there, he reached around my waist, impossibly climbing up the wall with me in his arms.

The others had already gone over and were racing for the wood line. I could see Darrell and his men following. I felt the heat of their fires at my back, and I suddenly wished I'd never come.

I watched anxiously as they ran for cover, then saw the enormous swarm that came out of the forest. They hadn't been far. I felt a pulse of relief.

Malcolm set me down. I turned to see our men and Darrell's, clashing together, fighting. Brother against brother. My knees buckled, and I collapsed onto the ground, struggling to breathe, holding my aching head in my hands. Pain engulfed me, and I couldn't move.

The noise of the battle was almost to much to take, I covered my ears. I knew we had to get going but I couldn't find the strength I needed to get back up on my feet.

The pulse was gone.

Two hands grasped my arms and pulled me up. I dragged my feet along as we headed back through the woods. A lonesome tribe of fairies, plus one human.

After a few hours of half-walking, I'd had enough. We could no longer hear the sounds of the battle raging behind us; I vaguely noticed that the children were tired. Probably more than just them, too. I let my legs stop and eased myself onto the ground. Malcolm looked at me curiously.

"Let's just rest for an hour," I heaved.

He nodded and motioned to let the others know.

I was already falling asleep.

CHAPTER ELEVEN

"Lady." Someone was shaking me. Ugh. "Lady, wake up. It's time to go."

Groaning, I sat up woozily and rubbed my eyes. I smacked my hand down on the ground and forced myself up before I could lie down again. The other fairies were just waking up. I tapped the feet of those who were still sleeping with the tip of my shoes.

"Wake up, wake up."

Leo met me in the center of camp.

"How did it go?"

"They retreated a few hours ago." He seemed smug. I couldn't blame him.

"Hours?" I pressed my hands against my back, it was sore from sleeping on the hard ground. "How long have we been here?"

"Most of the day, My Lady."

"Hm."

The fairies were all stumbling about now, struggling to wake up. What a sorry looking bunch they were. Bruises covered their skin; hollow eyes looked out of pale, gaunt faces. It was like I was leading a pack of the undead back to Erik's palace. I sighed; my hands automatically rose up to rest on my hips.

We started the walk back slowly. Leo and I walked with the crowd, neither of us talking.

Then, "Might I say, Lady Bethany, you did exceedingly well last night."

I smiled at him wearily. "Thank you. From the looks of things, you didn't do so bad yourself."

"True. Although," he sighed. "Darrell did slip through my fingers. I had wanted to bring him in, but he evaded everything we had to throw at him."

"But you go got the Auyen city back?"

"In pieces, yes; we have some men inside the city to guard it while we take these ones back to Aryan."

I glanced behind us, noticing only then that our military had been halved. "Casualties?"

"None this time, thanks to you. They weren't expecting us."

I chuckled to myself. "Just so long as you know, next time it's not going to be so easy. They won't underestimate us like that again."

"We'll be prepared for that."

"Good." I paused to pick up a dirty-faced, blue-eyed little girl. We three walked in silence for a long time. "Will we be back in time, you think?"

"I think so, maybe half a day late at the most."

I nodded. That was good. Erik wouldn't have much time to panic, then. We stopped again as the sun was going down, to eat, but the break didn't last very long. The spies had already gone ahead to relay the good news, and all we wanted was to be behind safe walls again. I didn't trust our safety to last long out here. I couldn't help looking over my shoulder, expecting to see Darrell and a new group of men coming to get us. I frowned and tried to think of other things.

We walked all that evening and for half of the night. The next day we got up late and started again, though much more slowly than the day before. The prisoners were so ill and weak that I worried some of them would die before we got to the palace. I made sure we stopped more often. My heart leaped when, on the third day, I caught sight of the familiar rushing river. Not much longer now and I would be back at the palace. Anticipation ate at my nerves, till we finally broke through the tree line.

Several women dressed in bright clothes spotted us in the distance and ran inside, shrieking excitedly. Leo and I exchanged smiles. I saw Aryan run out and watched him mentally tabulate the number of ill—which accounted for all of the prisoners—then watched him turn around and go back inside. I frowned. *Thanks a lot, doc.*

The women ran back out; they met us in the center of the enormous lawn and took up the small ones in their arms.

The nurse that had helped me touched my arm. "Go inside, Lady. We'll take it from here."

"Thank you."

I went inside, and, sighing, walked up to Mia's room. She was just coming out when I rounded the corner.

"Bethany, you're back!"

I nodded. "With every single captive—and we won back the city as well."

"Goodness..."she started, but then she saw the look on my face; she laughed softly. "But I suppose you want something to eat, and then get some rest."

I nodded again, too tired to speak. My lungs ached painfully.

She showed me where the kitchen was, across the wide house. We sat in there and I told her everything that had happened the night we set out. I pulled the piece of paper out of my pocket and handed it to her, explaining where I found it. She looked it over solemnly, frowning.

"What is it?"

"I can't be sure—I don't know what it means." She put it away. "I'll consult the others about it later."

The cook set a plate full of delectable sweets in front of me. I popped the first one in my mouth and looked at her, squinting.

"Did you ever find Daniel?"

"No, and we can't figure out who was with him. No one else in the court is missing." She flashed a glance at me. "Are you sure you weren't imagining it?"

I was insulted. "No, I was not."

"Just making sure." She shrugged.

"You should have more faith in me."

After I had eaten, she led the way out of the kitchen, into the yard. We crossed a wide space of greenery, finally coming upon a long white marble castle hidden behind the trees. It was handsome, with designs etched into the window and doors. Pink roses grew all around it, and the walk was completely made up of fairy moss. Mia opened the front door.

"This is where the Ladies stay," she told me. And we entered a round homey room, I looked around at the beautiful furniture, as I followed her down the hallway. She opened one door into a pretty, white and pink room with flowing curtains and an enormous bed. "Welcome home."

I took a step, then turned back. "You'll let me know when the next meeting is, won't you?"

"Absolutely."

I collapsed into the bed as soon as she'd gone. Though I wished desperately for sleep, my body was too tense. Flashes of the battle bounced behind my eyelids. I sighed and got out of bed. I took a long bath, washed my hair, and changed into a pretty red gown with sequins on the bodice.

I didn't explore the house—I didn't dare, considering the trouble I'd gotten into the last time. Instead, I went out.

The sun was hot and welcoming. I walked down through the forest to the river. I found a rock large enough to sit on and plunked myself down upon it, dipping my feet into the refreshing, cool water.

"Congratulations," a soft voice surprised me. I spun around; Erik was standing behind me, hands in his pockets. "I hear you've been quite the heroine."

"Glad you let me go now, huh?" I replied, a half smile stretching across my face.

He sat next to me, taking no notice of my teasing. "I was worried…"

"You don't have to worry about me, Erik. I can take care of myself. I always have."

"I know. Still, it was…difficult to let you go, even though you were right about that being the reason I came to you. I didn't have any other revenues…I wouldn't have put your life in danger otherwise." He seemed ashamed of himself, for some reason.

"Is Leo satisfied with me?"

"Seems to be."

The hot sun was scorching. I waved my hand to cool myself off, patting the water with my bare feet. I tried to think of something else to say that didn't have anything to do with the war.

Something greasy, sticky and wet wrapped around my ankle under the water. I couldn't see it, but it was clutching my ankle so tightly hurt. Before I could scream, it yanked on my foot.

I hit the water.

I bobbed up a couple seconds later, gasping. I spun around in the water, frantically trying to see where it went.

It was gone. Erik had jumped in beside me and was dragging me out of the water, his expression bleak.

"What…was…that….?" I coughed.

"I don't know." He looked down into the water. Nothing moved beneath the waves. I leaned away from it, shuddering.

He pulled me to my feet. "Maybe we'd better go…."

I followed behind him quickly. When I saw his face, I realized something.

"It's *not* funny."

"Yes, it is." He laughed. I ripped my hand away, placing it on my hip and glaring at him.

"You should have seen your face," he chortled. I rolled my eyes.

"Who knew someone so old could be so immature."

SOMEHOW, I FINALLY got up the courage to explore my new house that I now shared with the other Ladies. Though I'd met a few in the hall, I didn't know any of their names and hoped I wouldn't run across them during my adventure. After breakfast that morning, I quickly got dressed, combed my hair, and left my room. I paused outside the door. No one was in the hall.

I felt like a thief, sneaking around the way I was in broad daylight. I pushed the feeling away and went up the hall, treading silently on the light-colored carpet. I passed the various rooms, and then entered a wide opening before a flight of stairs. This is where the carpet ended, replaced by shining white glass. I stepped onto it lightly and opened the first door I came to.

It was a small parlor. There were five fairy women, consulting together, there. They stopped talking to look at me. I smiled timidly.

One, a young fairy with pretty silver hair and pointed ears, patted the seat beside her.

"Come on in, dear," her voice was welcoming.

"We were wondering when you would come venturing out," another interjected, smiling behind her fan.

"I-I've...been busy," I muttered, sitting down on the sofa.

"Well, we know *that*, but you know the Empire isn't all war and death and such. I'm beginning to fear that's the only part of it you've come to know."

I narrowed my eyes at her words, wondering if they were meant as an insult.

"Don't you girls think we should introduce ourselves to Lady Bethany?" The eldest of the group asked pointedly.

"Oh, yes." The fairy girl beside me pressed a small hand to her heart. "I'm Anita," then she proceeded to point around the room. "And that's Eve, Jade, Mimi, and Nikita."

I smiled, and gave them all a tiny wave. "Hi."

They nodded graciously.

And then Nikita spoke up. "Lady Bethany, I'm curious. What's it like being a royal favorite?"

I blushed. "I didn't know that I was."

"Oh...of course you are!" They laughed. "Do you think King Erik treats everyone the way he does you, dear?" She giggled, flicking her curly brown hair over her shoulder and looking about the room.

I pressed my hands together nervously. "I suppose I've been a bit too busy to notice that as well."

"Somehow I find that odd."

"And yet, if your good king and I hadn't worked as hard as we have been, we wouldn't have just saved the Auyen city the other day, now would we?"

They were silent, for a moment, looking a lot like frightened little birds.

"She does have a point," Jade murmured, fanning herself.

Mimi tittered. "All the same. Some good old-fashioned socializing never killed anyone."

I just smiled and nodded. I'd never met a sillier group of women in all my life.

CHAPTER TWELVE

It was twilight; the sun long gone and the stars just beginning to shine. I was heading for the meeting, the captive girl known as Nina ambling at my side. Her story was one of many we purposed to hear tonight. Why, I didn't know. But Erik seemed to think we might get something useful from their stories—clues to Darrell's strategy, perhaps?

I shook my head. To me it was sheer cruelty to take a horror someone had just escaped and make them relive it.

Nina reminded me of Vivian. She had long hair, sweet dark eyes, and a mouth that seemed to perpetually smile, even when she wasn't completely happy. I felt a connection to her from the moment I'd met her.

She told me that her father was the governor of the city—had been. Darrell killed him in the initial attack. Apparently, he had been fighting on the front line. I felt a pull at this—no leader should be at the front lines of a battle.

Maybe I only felt that way because I could never even imagine Erik standing in the front lines, although I knew he would most happily do so. I shuddered away from the thought. We were close to the delegates' housing now, I hurried to the door, eager to get away from my own thoughts. I opened the heavy wooden door and stood aside for Nina.

She held back and, at first, I thought it was because she was nervous—reluctant to be on with it. But then she turned her soulful eyes to me and motioned slowly with her hand. I understood then. From the time I had saved her from the other side, I had reached a level of the hierarchy that was above hers...maybe that'd always been the case, and I just didn't see it.

We were early getting to the room, but Erik, Leo, and several guards whom I recognized were all there. As soon as I opened the door, the room burst into a fit of clapping.

They were all looking at me. I blushed at glanced accusingly at Leo, who just kept it up, laughing loudly.

Erik was sitting in a chair at the head of the long brown table. He motioned to the chair beside him with his hand.

I patted Nina on the arm encouragingly then went to my seat. Across from me, on the other side of Erik sat a fairy with long black hair. Glistening spots ran across his cheek bones and down his throat.

I'd never seen a fairy with facial markings before....

Erik placed a hand on my knee, and I stopped my staring, hoping that he was the only one who had noticed. I looked down, ashamed of having broken etiquette. My cheeks burned. Erik made them quiet down, then, and the meeting began.

It was awful. We sat there for hours, listening to the grievances of the captive fairies, asking questions that they couldn't answer without breaking down, and then—once they had been dismissed by a gentle wave of the king's hand—trying to figure out just what Darrell's pattern was.

I had to point out that he might not have one at all. He might be plundering cities randomly, causing destruction solely for the chaos. If he had no set plan, barring the destruction of Empire property, then we really couldn't know when he would strike again, or *where* he would. I wondered if we could possibly get any spies into his army; Mia told me they were working on it.

After about six hours of this, my backside grew numb. I squirmed around in the chair, trying to find solace for my aching lower spine. I caught Erik smirking, though he wouldn't look at me directly. I ignored him.

Then, the strange, glistening fairy spoke up. His voice was surprisingly deep and kind. "We've done enough of this wandering about, trying to understand our enemy. We already know from our history that fairies of his like are heartless, and cunning. He does not care about the losses—not even on his side—so long as he gets what he wants. I say we quit sitting around this table like a bunch of toads and do something." He looked at me and motioned with his hand. "What else, is she for?"

Beside me, Erik stiffened. I snuck a glance at his rigid visage and dropped my eyes again. I didn't like where this was going.

"Did His Majesty not bring her here for a reason?" the fairy continued angrily. "She's proven herself useful already. Surely, with her help we won't fail."

"I don't like the point you're trying to put across, Colonel," Erik snapped, speaking for the first time in a little while. The sound of his voice made me jump.

"No, but you understand it. Our people can't wait any longer, Your Majesty. Your generals like to think too much, and it's beginning to wear on me, and the people of my city."

"What? You think we can just hop into a battle and get away with it, with our lives?" one fairy hissed.

"I'm saying the cost if we don't will be higher." With that, he stood, bowed stiffly, and left. It was an act that—even with all its blatant insubordination and ill-bidding— left me in awe.

THE MORNING, I WENT with a search party to look for Darrell. Leo was convinced he and his pack of thieves were hiding out in the woods somewhere, and he was doggedly determined not to lost their trail.

After several long hours of walking, we returned to the scene of the battle. Leo guided me around it, keeping his hand on my eyes as though I were a child. I didn't argue, I had dreaded the sight the whole trip over...And the smell was bad enough.

We went in the direction some soldiers had seen Darrell run, and began our search with the river. We split up; half took the right side, half took the left. I went out on my own.

The trees were dark and ominous today, swaying in the wind and groaning loudly as their old trunks protested the movement. I wondered how Leo ever expected to find Darrell in a place like this, when the vines were so thickly intertwined with the trees and shrubs that a person couldn't see more than two feet ahead of her, and the high ferns covered every inch of ground. I was certain we would find nothing here.

Yet I inched my way along, bending the ferns with my hands, to see below them and tripping on the occasional root. It was harder the further we went, because then we had the vines to contend with. Some fairies resorted to cutting them down, while I merely shoved them as far out of the way as I was able. If Darrell was here, I wanted to leave no sign that I'd been through.

As we progressed, the forest grew darker and quieter. I couldn't tell if this was because we were getting tired, or because something sinister was going on around my little unsuspecting troupe.

It was a long, mundane process. We covered more than ten miles going one way, and then after I'd rested, we had to come back. As we returned, we continued to search the area for clues. We were nearly out of the thick of it, when someone yelled to the West of us.

All around me began the thunder of feet, as fairies ran towards the sound. I ran too and was the last to arrive. Leo pushed me back slightly with a gentle hand. I strained to see what was going on.

Two fairies leaned over something in the dirt. It was a small leather bag, tied at the end with a string of the same material. Leo picked it up. He opened and sniffed it. "Poison," he stated. I felt the blood freeze in my chest; I'd been through this way and I knew that nothing had been there before. I looked up into the trees. They revealed nothing.

The hairs on the back of my neck stood up, sending chills through me. Something was wrong.

"Are we through here?" I heard myself ask him. I don't know why I said that, I hadn't meant to. Even though I really did want to get away from these woods terribly.

Leo stuffed the poison into his bag as he rose to his feet. "Getting tired, Lady Bethany?"

"No, of course not."

He laughed. "We're nearly done. Don't worry, we'll be back soon."

By the evening, I was back home. At least, that's what I called it now. Home. I sighed and wondered if I'd ever be back in good old Oregon again. My heart twanged in my chest. For a fleeting second, I honestly doubted it.

I ran my hand over my face, I couldn't think like that; I wouldn't survive.

A knock at the door made me leap into the air.

"Lady Bethany?"

"Yes?" I didn't recognize the voice.

"His Majesty would like to speak to you."

What could Erik want *now*? I frowned and got up off the bed. I opened the door, still frustrated.

"Why"—I caught my breath. Daniel.

He grabbed my arm and yanked me through the doorway. I jerked back.

"Let go of me!" I struggled to get away from him, but he ignored me.

Daniel pulled me down the hallway, even as I struggled to pull away from him. I dug my fingernails deep into the skin of his hand and tried to kick at his feet. My chest thundered, but no strength went to my limbs. I wanted to throw up. Something was wrong. Daniel didn't have any trouble dragging me down the long corridor.

I kicked at his thigh desperately, trying to trip him. To throw him off balance. Instantly, he spun around and snapped my arm back. He wrapped his fingers around my hands so tightly I expected to hear the bones snap.

"You should behave yourself, Lady. You're at my mercy now," he hissed. My eyes flashed wildly at his sarcastic use of the word. I ripped my wrists back. Daniel didn't let go.

"No, I'm *not!*"

Daniel laughed at me; when he started to drag me down the stairs, I bit his fingers. He gasped loudly, then, unexpectedly, his arm snapped forward, and his hands let go of me.

Suddenly, my body was airborne, but only briefly. Pain exploded in my side when I hit the corners of the stairs. My body tumbled down, each step stabbing me in the sides and shoulders and hips with sharp jabs. I landed at the bottom with a grunt.

You have to get up, I told myself. I tried to move my head; everything was bleary. The world spun on its side and I squeezed my eyes shut, trying to fight the panic. If I didn't move now, Daniel was going to kill me. I turned my face to the other side and slid my hands underneath me. Where was the pulse? I didn't understand why it was gone.

Daniel grabbed my hands and ripped me up off the ground. He flung me around so that I was facing the door and pushed me onward.

Just then, the door opened, and the Colonel appeared in the doorway. Seeing my condition, he glared down at Daniel, his face turning an odd shade of reddish purple.

Daniel stared back. A moment passed, but no one moved. Then, the Colonel reached out and took hold of my shoulder. He pulled me away from Daniel, but the rogue tried to hold onto me.

Maintaining his hold on my shoulder, he punched Daniel in the jaw with his right hand. Instantly, I was released.

"Go."

I ran across the lawn. My lungs burned, but I hardly noticed them as I raced towards the palace doors.

Erik was just coming out when I got there. He stared at me in surprise.

"Bethany! I'd have thought you'd be resting."

"I...was...ran...into...trouble." I heaved, leaning over on my knees to keep from toppling over. Some warrior princess I was. "Daniel," I spat out.

Instantly, my feet were lifted off the ground; Erik carried me inside and placed me on a red velvet couch, he knelt beside me. "Where?"

"At my room. He tried to take me away. The Colonel"—

Just then the door opened, and the Colonel walked in. "We have Daniel in custody, your Majesty."

"Good." Erik's tone was bleak. "Throw him where he belongs and don't let me hear of him again."

The Colonel shot me a look. "Are you all right?"

I nodded. He didn't look convinced.

"I heard you fall. You were toppling down those stairs at a good speed, my lady. Maybe you should have Aryan look at you."

I sat up straighter. "I'm fine, thank you, sir. I don't need a doctor any more than I did before."

He smiled. Turned.

"Colonel," Erik said.

The Colonel turned his head to the side but didn't turn. He merely awaited the remainder of the message.

Erik was looking at me, his blue eyes tranquil; his words were lethal. "I want the other one found."

"I already sent the scouts out."

"Excellent."

He walked out of the room, and I heard the door shut a few seconds later. Erik went over to the window. He stood there for a long time, staring out, his hands clasped behind his back.

"What is it?"

"Everything. Ever since you came here you've been faced with one thing after another, and I can't seem to get a hold on it."

"Well this is a war, isn't it?"

"Yes, but I hadn't expected you would be such a target. For your own side, I mean."

I leaned back. The cushions felt good against my sore back. "I'm your secret weapon, remember? Of course, I'm going to be a target."

He turned to me, a smile curling up one side of his mouth. "Yes...and you've done wonders for us already. It's the outcome I'm worried about."

"What do you mean, exactly?" I asked politely.

"Don't you remember what your mother told you about the moon?"

I nodded. Of course, I did; the words reverberated through my mind. "She said it meant bad things for the friend of fairies."

His eyes shifted a shade darker, he nodded grimly.

"Oh no." My blood went cold.

"Now you understand," he said, his voice broke.

"Yes."

"I don't think we'll be able to escape our troubles, Bethany. You or I." He turned to the window again, biting his lip.

"Well, now, I'm worried too." I stood up and crossed my arms over my chest. "But I'm not going to let it get in my way."

He turned towards me, taken aback. "Bethany, this isn't your responsibility. These aren't your people."

"They look up to me now, Erik. I can't let them down."

"You can't stay here, either, if it means death for you."

"How do you know that it does? Don't tell me you're one of those silly, superstitious types." Though I myself had worried about the color of the moon on some nights, it embarrassed me to think of how seriously I'd taken it. My cheeks burned slightly at the memory.

"I'm not going to let things like that rule my life and neither are you. We're going to work at this together, and we're going to win this war *together* whether you like it or not. I don't see why you're worrying about this now anyway. You're the one who came to me in the first place, remember?"

"I've done a lot of things in the past I shouldn't have done—that's not the least of them."

I rolled my eyes. "You know what? I don't even care. I'll do it myself if you're not up to it."

He turned on me, anger hardening his eyes. "I never said that."

"Sure seems like you're trying to." I threw my hands in the air. "So what? My life's been threatened. It's war, that's what happens. There's no way of getting around it. Deal with it. I am."

"But you're not the one that will have to live with the consequences if you die."

"I'm not going to die."

"How do you know?"

"How do you know I will?" He didn't say anything, and I smiled.

"And what about what happened this morning?"

I frowned. "What?"

"The poison they found. Leo told me. He told me what they saw, too."

"I didn't know they saw anything."

"Darrell. Tagging along behind *you*."

I sighed. I sat down on the couch again, all my confidence deflated. "Why did you ask me here, just out of curiosity?"

"Mia wanted it. She knew I'd been keeping an eye on things...you...when I told her that you were the only one that could help us, she talked me into going through the veil to get you. I didn't want to...I never would have, if the stakes hadn't been so high...they already were too high—for you. I didn't want to have any part in what might happen to you here. "

"How did she convince you, then?"

He sat down. "She reminded me that I wasn't the only fairy royal looking into your life."

"Darrell was watching me?"

"Of course, he was. You have the potential for great things in this kingdom, and he wanted you for himself. That's why I, in turn, kept an eye on you as well. I wanted to make sure he stayed out of your life." He sighed. "Once I got there, I really didn't have a *choice* but to bring you with me. Darrell would have snatched you up the moment I left."

"How come everyone else seems to think I'm this great warrior princess and I don't?"

Erik smiled faintly, but his face was drawn. "Because you are. That's your nature. I don't think you've ever taken adequate recognition for the things you've done in your life. You've been much too busy leaning on Tracy and Marissa."

"I do not lean on them."

"Yes, you do. You distract yourself from your own life and problems by watching theirs and calling them to come to the rescue when you think you need them. They always come. And you never have to deal with anything on your own. Until now." He looked at the carpet.

I shook my head. "That's not true."

But he just looked up at me, his liquid azure eyes were more compelling than any argument. I got up and headed for the door.

"Where are you going?"

"I don't know, to walk around."

He caught up to me. "Care if I come?"

"Only if you insist on being a pessimist."

"I won't then."

We went out into the cool early morning air. Something occurred to me, and I asked him. "How big is the Empire, exactly?"

He told me, seeming surprised by the sudden change of subject.

I thought about that, about all the fairies and cities that could be contained in that wide range....and Darrell's small band of men.

It clicked then, what Erik had told be and what I read in the history books. It all meant one thing.

He was recruiting my people.

"Bethany?"

"Erik. I know how he's doing it now!" I told him, and his brow furrowed.

"Are you sure?"

"Positive." I thought back. "I remember, a couple of kids went missing in Washington last year. It was a weird case because there was no evidence, nothing to even suggest what could have happened." I frowned. "I bet that was him."

"Even so, it was tricky enough to get you here—"

"Yeah, but he's been doing it for years. He's got it down to a science by now. I'm the first person that you've ever brought across."

"He never tried to take you, though. You're the only one worth bringing."

"Which can only mean one thing...." I trailed off, watching, waiting for him to figure it out himself. His eyes lit.

"I have to talk to Mia and Leo."

"Go ahead. I'll be over there."

"No, you won't; you're coming with me. The other one is still loose, remember?"

I rolled my eyes. "Erik, the palace grounds are full of fairy mommies and their babies, no one's going to try to get to me now."

"Fine," he relented, "just stay out of trouble."

I followed the river along the rose garden, thinking. It didn't take long for me to decide I didn't want to think about Darrell and his fairy slash human army. Its implications were far too difficult for me to process at the moment. I ran my hands over the rows of rose bushes lightly. It seemed so strange to me that a world so beautiful could produce so much horror and death.

Of course, Erik did say that this is the first the Empire has had in thousands of years. I guessed I should give them some credit for that. It was Darrell that was pushing them to the edge; they obviously didn't want anything to do with it. It showed in their hesitations, their long drawn-out meetings. Everything. Everything they did they did slowly, to stall and put off the battle scene. The Colonel was right when he told them they were wasting time. Better to get it done and over with.

An icy wind blew past me; I shuddered. I looked back towards the palace but didn't see Erik.

Maybe I should have gone with him. To explain for myself.

I twirled around, the breeze catching the ruffles on my dress, and floating them through the air. I smiled.

A tall willow-like tree jutted out of the ground, ahead of me. I sauntered towards it, taking my time. I could hear the shouts of little fairies in the distance. I roamed through the rose bushes and thorns to the end of the lawn, pressing on through the tall grass and the young saplings, careful not to step on a snake. Something at the back of my mind told me I was going too far without someone with me, but I ignored it. I wasn't afraid.

My sides ached, reminding me of Daniel. What if his friend was out here somewhere?

I hit a road and stepped onto it, turning right and walking alongside the rising sun. I walked for miles, lost in thought. The only thing that pulled me from my reverie was the sudden realization that I had entered a little town.

Dark-haired fairies were everywhere, carrying baskets and pushing carts. I saw a young mother and her tiny son, sitting at a doorstep. They both looked up as I passed, then went back to their game of fairy patty cake. I bought two oranges, sweet pieces of fruit with the money Mia had given me and walked back the way I had come. I took my time. I didn't have to be anywhere, and I wanted to see how the meeting went, anyway.

But Erik hadn't come back yet when I reached the palace. I sighed heavily, and plunked myself down on the ground, rolling the fruit around in my hand, and gazing off into the garden. I ate slowly and tried to keep my mind off my impatience by picking a pile of tall wildflowers. I stripped them of their petals and made an attempt to braid them all into a little basket. It was harder than I'd thought it would be, after about an hour or so the best I had was a messy knot. I took it apart and started over again, taking another bite as I did.

I heard someone walking close to me and looked up. It was him, I smiled. "Well?"

His eyes were tired, but Erik smiled down at me. "Well what? What are you doing on the ground?"

I frowned. "Trying to make a basket. It's not working out for me so well, though. I don't think I can do it."

Unexpectedly, he grabbed my arm and pulled me off the ground gently, trying not to hurt my sides. "We're going to block the hole."

"What hole?"

"There's a very thick veil between my world and yours. The only way anyone can get through it is through the hole. It's been there for as long as our history records...no one really knows how it got there; it certainly wasn't an accident....But if we can close it, that should cut him off from your world."

My heart skipped a beat.

"But then how will I get back?"

He exhaled. "That's just it, Bethany. I can't make any assurances that after the hole is closed we'll be able to open it again. I understand perfectly if you want to cross realms beforehand."

I thought about it. Leaving would mean I could be with my mother again, and Marissa, and especially Tracy. I wanted to go back so badly it hurt. If I went back I could finish school and go to college like I had always wanted to...get that job I had always wanted....But even though I still wanted all that, the picture it painted seemed empty, bleak and colorless.

I shook my head a little bit as we ambled through the huge rooms. I had no idea where we were going. I didn't think about it.

I couldn't leave them. Excepting those fairies that still thought I was a danger to the Empire, which were few, I was like a superhero to them. If I left, I had a feeling that everything would fall apart. Plus, I wouldn't be able to live with myself if I didn't finish what I'd started. I'd feel like a quitter, a failure. Not to mention the fact that Erik counted on me...

"No," I murmured finally. "No, I can't do that."

He nodded slowly, blue eyes watching my expression. "We'll try to get you back as soon as possible, Bethany."

I took a deep breath, and made myself smile at him, feeling a wrench in my chest for what I could be giving up. "Let's take these things as they come, okay? We have enough problems to worry about without trying to figure out how you're going to cart me back."

"All the same, we will." There was something in his face, something else that he was keeping from me. I narrowed my eyes.

"Is there something else?"

His eyes widened. "No," he answered in a light tone. "Nothing at all. That's all that we talked about."

I stared at him for a second, then turned to the door. "What's behind here?" I shoved it open.

It was the smallest chamber I'd seen. The walls were all light-colored and carved beautifully in ancient artwork. I ran my fingers over the wall, marveling. There was a great big window in the center of the room, but its pale blue curtains were closed. They let in an eerie bright blue light. It filled the room, and yet, somehow, shaded it as well. To the left stood a short bookcase filled with reading material, and many scrolls. And in the center of the room, there was an odd piece of furniture; it stood on three dramatically carved, dark wooden legs, the top seemed to be made of glass and it resembled a dark bulb.

I turned to Erik and raised my eyebrows.

He shut the door. "Follow me." Erik took my wrist and led me to the center of the room, where the thing stood. He raised my hand, and moved it in the air, from side to side—the way I had with the lamp several days ago but without my fingers touching the glass.

Slowly, the glass changed. It fogged over, then darkened as a gloomy, familiar landscape came into focus.

It was my home. My mother had just returned from work and was getting out of her car. I watched, breathless, as the lens shifted again, and I was suddenly staring into a small dorm room.

My sister sat on the bed, notebook in hand, looking extremely frustrated as she leaned over her work. I felt a bit jealous, watching her struggle with the questions.

Then the glassy bulb misted over and went dark.

"One more?" I pleaded. Erik smiled and shook his head.

"You have an appointment to keep."

"What appointment? With who? I don't want to."

"Aryan is not going to let you do anything else until he's certain you're all right."

"I'm all right," I tried to sound firm, but he wouldn't listen.

"Well, it won't hurt to make sure of it, come on now."

I went to the door with him and waited as he stopped to lock it. "Why do I have the feeling this is all your fault?"

Erik made a face.

CHAPTER THIRTEEN

For the next month, they worked on closing the gap between our worlds. Darrell continued to provoke the kingdom. Somehow, he seemed to know all our weak spots, always attacking the most vulnerable cities, ransacking them, and then leaving them behind, barren long before we could get there. During this time, Erik sunk into a depression; despite everything he'd done for his subjects, he'd labeled himself a failure. A king incapable of protecting his people from his own brother.

Then, one day Mia burst through the door of my room. Her eyes glowed with excitement, and her cheeks were pink.

I was kneeling before my miniature library, looking for something else to read. I'd already found a book earlier, but I wanted to find one that didn't involve so much killing. I frowned at her flushed complexion; Mia never blushed. "What?"

"We've done it! We've closed the hole!"

I felt my heart sink, and my face went with it. This was not welcome news. All this time, I'd been hoping that they wouldn't be able to complete the task. It was selfish, of course, but I didn't savor the thought of being cut off from my own universe. The thought that I might be forever cut off from my mother and sister made my eyes sting.

Mia's eyes dimmed as she saw my expression. I tried to recover, pushing my lips into a stiff smile as I got off the floor. "Great!" I tried to sound enthusiastic, to mask my disappointment. Mia beamed at my enthusiasm. "That didn't take long."

"Our men wouldn't take long if they think they can seal him out somewhere."

"That's not what we're...." I snorted. "Mia!"

She laughed. "We had to get them to move fast." She shrugged. "I just told them whatever popped into my head. Besides, at the time, there *was* a chance."

I shrugged. "Well, it worked. I guess. But what happens when someone sees him?"

"Time travels fast."

"It sure seems to." I looked down at the thick blue novel on my bed.

"Don't worry, Lady Bethany."

"Hmm?" My brow furrowed. I raised my eyes to her face, still caressing the cover of the book with my fingertips. The motion calmed me somehow.

She was watching me. "We'll get the portal open again once this is over; you'll see."

I nodded. Sighed. Wondered what to do now.

"Aren't you hungry?"

I shook my head. "Cecil stuffed me this morning. I don't think I'll be able to eat for at least a couple more days." Mia laughed at the face I made.

"Oh well. I'm eating..." she turned quickly and hopped through the threshold.

Once Mia was out of sight, I deflated. I was close to the edge of a panic. I ran my hands through my hair. What to do, what to do...I had to keep my mind off it. I grabbed the book and went out.

The sultry air caressed my bare forearms and face. Untimely darkness covered the palace grounds; I looked up, trying to find the sun somewhere behind huge, blackish clouds. A violent wind spun the treetops in a circular fashion, but I never even felt a breeze.

"Hmm." Was this because we closed the hole?

It may not be the best idea to read out here, after all. But the thought of going back to my room was unthinkable.

So long as I stayed close, in case a storm broke out, I should be okay. I found a nice soft spot near the trees and sat down. This book was much better than the one I'd had before and I quickly fell into step with the plot, completely engrossed.

It felt like seconds later I felt something behind me. I looked over my shoulder, half-expecting to see someone coming up to me. But there was no one. I tried to read some more. The sense that I was not alone gradually grew stronger and stronger, until the presence weighed heavily on my back. It was suffocating. It reminded me of the darkness that had followed me before I came to this world. I scrambled to my feet, panic making me jumpy. I couldn't *see* anything.

I heard the rush of plants moving. And then Erik was beside me, glaring into the woods. He grabbed me by the arm and dragged me back towards the palace. Several guards raced past us towards the forest, shouting orders.

I stumbled sideways, trying to see what was going on. Erik jerked my arm. I whirled around again to look at his face. It was fierce, and wary. He never so much as glimpsed down at me.

"What's going on?"

Erik didn't speak. We'd reached the doorway now, and I set my feet hard against the ground. I wasn't going anywhere until he told me what was happening.

He just picked me up and put me inside, shutting the door behind him.

"Erik!"

Mia appeared, seemingly out of thin air. She bowed low.

I felt a spark of hope. Certainly, she would tell me what all the commotion was about. I didn't like the anxiety I felt emanating from Erik.

"Go with the others. Bring her back," he ordered, cutting me off. His voice was gruff.

"Yes, Your Majesty." Mia ducked her head and sashayed out, glancing up at me once furtively.

I glared. "What *happened*?"

"Darrell sent some of his men here."

"Well, then I should be out there!" I struggled, trying to writhe out of his grasp. He wouldn't let me. I glared up at his handsome face, frustrated. A strange look haunted his eyes, it sent chills down my spine.

"Not this time," Erik told me. "I don't want you out there."

"But—" Something was wrong. There was something he wasn't telling me.

One of the guards came running down the hall. Before I could ask any more questions, Erik handed me to him. "Keep her inside."

"You're not going out there?" My voice sounded as incredulous as I felt. Surely, he wouldn't be going in without me.

Erik didn't answer. He turned on his heel and went out, slamming the door behind him. I stood there, frozen beside the young fairy. He tugged on me gently, and I followed him into the parlor, feeling anything but resigned. I went straight to the window; the soldiers and generals were arriving, swarming towards the wood line. Erik was there, with them, right in front.

My heart lurched with jealousy and worry. It was an odd emotion—I was torn between the two.

"Why is he doing this to me?" I whined to the young fairy standing at the door.

"He is only trying to protect you, My Lady."

I shook my head. "Foolishness." I bit my lip. I was starting to sound like Nikita.

He didn't reply.

I watched as the herd of fairies with their weapons raised and waving wrathfully vanished into the woods. I pressed my lips together and put a hand to my forehead. When I opened my eyes, my young guard was standing completely still, hands clasped in front of him, before the open doorway.

I glared at him through narrowed eyes. "What am I—a prisoner?"

His face was smooth as glass. "His Majesty wished for you to stay inside, My Lady."

"I'm not going anywhere."

Something flashed through his eyes, then. I couldn't tell what it was, but I suspected he thought I was lying. "What's your name?"

"Arthur, my Lady," he answered, leaning slightly forward as he spoke.

"Arthur." I turned to the window again. "Well, Arthur. Your king is insane."

He sounded entertained when he spoke again. "You know you're the only one that can speak and act towards him the way you do."

"I think I'm the only one who's dared," I responded remotely.

"Even the general doesn't."

"Mia?"

He nodded slowly.

"Hm....And I suppose you think it's disrespectful?" I asked, not looking at him. He made a sound—like he was going to say something, and then changed his mind. I turned my eyes to him evenly. His expression was fearful, torn. I smirked. Usually fairies were not so afraid of me.

Maybe I looked as dangerous as I felt. Good.

A muffled explosion caught my attention then, and I tensed. I swayed my head from side to side, trying to see through the thick green wall ahead of me. It was impossible. I gripped the windowpane tightly and groaned. Adrenaline coursed through my body, though I wasn't in danger at the moment. I fidgeted nervously and turned away from the window, pacing back and forth from one end of the long room to the other. Arthur watched me calmly. This was so unfair.

I might have to kill him. I folded my arms behind my back and walked fast.

It went on forever. Once Arthur offered to get me something, though how he thought I'd be able to eat was beyond me. I told him no and kept on pacing, pausing periodically to gaze out the window, though it never did me any service. I'd have gone to the secret room and used the mirror, but I knew Arthur would follow me.

I groaned, finally tired of being watched. "I'm going to my room."

I stalked back with Arthur on my tail and slammed my door in his face.

Relief flooded me the second the door was between us. I ran my hands through my hair and turned towards the little sofa.

Darrell was sitting in my window. He stared at me in silence, his green eyes enigmatic.

I clenched my fist. "How did you get in here?"

He scoffed. "Does that matter? I've come to steal you away." He took a step forward and I, a step back. I wrenched the door open again.

Arthur stared at me, shocked.

Darrell's form was flying across the room. Somehow, I caught his ankle with my foot and yanked it sideways. He tumbled to the floor, taking me with him.

And then Arthur was there. I heard the crunch of bone against bone when he punched him. Darrell fell sideways.

My world grew dark, and the floor dropped out from underneath me. My chest rattled with gritty, fiery bursts and my mind went blank. Someone grabbed my arms and drew me carefully off the carpet. I was drowning in adrenaline and couldn't stop shaking. I barely noticed the two other fairies that passed us to help Arthur.

What happened next, I didn't see. I was led down the hall and into the parlor, gasping and crying. I heard someone say something about the stress.

It wasn't the stress. It was the fact that I had just realized my life was going to be endanger for every second I remained here. And now, the tear in the Veil had been closed. I must stay, regardless of what may happen.

THE SUN WAS SETTING in the sky when they came back. I raced to the window at the sound of their return. My heart jolted as I watched the soldiers stumble across the lawn. Their armor was torn and battered and dirty; I saw blood covering their arms and faces.

What happened? Did we lose? My eyes searched the crowd for Erik, panicking. My heart banged around in my chest. He wasn't there. I whirled to face the door.

Arthur was already gone. He'd probably gone to help with the wounded already. I dashed outside and ran to them. The fairy women had beaten me to the crowd, assisting those that couldn't walk, or those that hardly could.

I raced through, examining the faces of the fairies. Half their number had not yet returned. Mia wasn't there, nor was Erik. But I saw Leo come limping through the woods.

I raced over to him, swinging his arm over my shoulder to support him as much as a frail human girl could. "What happened?"

"It was...an ambush...we lost most of our men out there." He groaned. "I don't know how we'll ever be able to recover from this."

My eyes were wide, I felt like screaming. What about Erik? What about Mia?

"Where is he?" I demanded. I looked back at the trees. I didn't see him among the stream of ravaged faces appearing from the forest. My hands started to shake.

Leo grunted in pain; I shifted my attention back to him. He was the color of exhaustion and agony. He huffed a little before answering, "Back there somewhere. I haven't seen him since he ordered the retreat. We got out of there as quickly as possible. I...had assumed he'd be the first one back."

I shook my head and motioned for a young fairy girl to come over. She met us and took hold of Leo's other arm. I let him go. "Take care of him."

"You'd better go find His Majesty, Bethany."

I nodded and pushed back through the crowd, into the forest. There still were a few stragglers coming through. I didn't know if that was good news or not. I hoped I could make it there in time. Many of the soldiers stopped when they saw me coming. When they saw where I was going they yelled for me to stop.

I ignored them all. I stumbled on the rocks and fallen trees, and on my dress. I yanked it around, holding out of the way so I could run. My sides stung and eventually I had to stop.

I didn't recognize where I was. My eyes were filled with tears and I couldn't see. I rubbed them away irately. Why Erik? *Why?*

He should have let me come. I ran away from the setting sun, until I hit a little meadow. Erik was struggling with three armed men. I saw Mia taking her chances with one of Darrell's generals.

I didn't break stride. Launching myself at them, I leaped on a fairy's back. I clawed at his eyes, too angry to pay attention to much else, yet I could feel the strange, pounding power building in my chest again. The feeling gave me confidence to augment the anger, I conquered my opponent quickly. I turned to another, working with Erik to bring him down.

A large colonel materialized before us. Instinctively, I snapped a sidekick into his belly, Erik knocked him over and plowed across the field to assist Mia.

I stayed put to grabble with someone else, knowing I wouldn't be able to reach her as fast.

The man kicked me in the stomach, and I reeled, landing hard on the ground. He towered above me, raising his axe-like weapon high in the air, a hideous expression on his face. I rolled just in time. It just missed me, slicing off a lock of my hair.

My heel smashed into his knee and as he fell, I hopped to my feet and hit him squarely on the head.

Erik and Mia were still fighting with the general. From what I could see of their fight, he was far more experienced than any other of Darrell's men. Faster.

I realized only then that this was one of the men Darrell had brought back with him from my world. How he got so fast, I didn't know. Maybe he had a talent like me....

I pushed the thoughts out of my mind and ran to meet up with them. I kicked him back and Erik took care of the rest. Mia leaned over onto her knees, swaying sideways, smiling at me wryly. I moved to support her.

Abruptly the meadow was enveloped in a deep silence. My sides and lungs stung; my knees felt weak. When Erik turned towards us, I reached out to him and hugged him.

"Next time..." I panted. "I....am...coming with you."

He patted my back but said nothing. I let him go. Three of our fairies limped into my line of sight.

"Let's go." Mia straightened up, staggered towards the palace. Erik and I followed slowly. We were on our guard, waiting for anyone who might be waiting—hiding.

"Are you all right?"

"I will be in a few minutes. You?"

My eyebrows met between my eyes. "Angry. Don't do that to me again."

"You're lucky I *didn't* let you go."

"I can't agree with that."

Erik sighed. "How many came back, do you know?"

I frowned at his less than subtle hint. "Leo says we lost more than half of the men that went out." I looked down, tripped on a root. Erik caught me.

I was too tired to argue with him. He wouldn't give in anyway, so there was no point. But, I told myself, the next time I would be going. Whether he liked it or not.

When we got back to the palace, we found Aryan's office overflowing with patients. He saw us come in and hurried over. He bowed.

"Your Highness," he stuttered. "We were worried..."

Erik held up a hand, impatience coloring his expression. "Just sew us up."

"Yes, Your Majesty, Your Grace....."

I giggled.

Erik did not look happy as Aryan stitched his arm. He stared into space, still and gloomy, till the doctor was finished, then stood. He walked past me and sauntered down the hallway without a glance in my direction.

I kissed Mia's head and followed him.

"Wait up!"

He stopped at the door. "Not now, Bethany, I have things to do."

"You're going to include me in them, then. I want to know what's going on."

"No, you don't."

"Is it Darrell?" I pressed. "Is there another hole? What?"

He shook his head. "The hole has been closed, there's no other."

"You're keeping something from me."

"Yes."

"Are you going to ever tell me?"

He sighed. "Just..."

I folded my arms across my chest and stared at him. Erik rubbed his eyes.

"Whatever." I gave up. I whirled around and stalked off to the sickroom.

CHAPTER FOURTEEN

Mia was just coming out when I got to the door. Her eyes dimmed when she saw my face. "Are you okay?"

"No, I'm not. I'm starting to wish I'd gone home when I had the chance." And then I went back to the house. Nina was in the parlor with the other ladies; she gave me a look I understood well. I couldn't help but smile.

"Do you want to take a walk with me?"

Nina nodded, relief clear on her face, and went to the door, waving shyly to the other girls as she went.

"Thank you," she murmured once we were outside.

I nodded. "Don't worry about it."

We walked in silence for a moment or two. I could hear the wailing outside the houses and frowned. My eyes burned. So much death, and pain. All because of me. My fault. I ran my hands through my hair, trying to disperse the feeling that they should be blood-soaked.

Yet, if I had decided to go home—if I hadn't even come at all—I wondered if I would have slept any better.

Nina looked back to the women. "We lost?" she demanded, breaking me out of my thoughts.

"Yes," I said matter-of-factly, waving my fan.

My expression caught her attention. Nina watched me questioningly, but I didn't want to tell her about my argument with her king.

"I don't understand. We've been doing so well, it seems...."

"Not this time."

She made a face. Why was I snapping at her for? It wasn't her fault. I sighed, suddenly exhausted.

We walked along the glassy sidewalks, breathing in air that was heavy with grief and anger. I don't think either of us really wanted to walk as far as we did. We probably wouldn't have, if not for the fact that the thought of going back inside made everything seem so much worse.

I tried to think of some way to fix it. To make things better. Even if I couldn't bring our men back, there had to be something that I *could* do. Something that would ease the burden.

I could think of nothing.

I TRIED THE NEXT DAY to get some food to make dinner. I couldn't get very far without someone coming up to me. The signs of our loss were everywhere, and it made me angrier. He should have taken me with him.

Women wiped away tears as they spoke to me, but the men were irate and dark. All of them looked at me, as though betrayed, wondering why I wasn't there to fight for them that day. And it was all because of him.

Why couldn't he just listen to me?

I tried my best to comfort those that approached me. I let their harsh words pass through my ears as though I hadn't heard. It wasn't easy. I went home early; although I didn't get everything I wanted that day, I did manage to get some. Enough, considering there were those who probably had much less.

Aryan was walking at the water's edge.

"Aryan?"

He looked up, startled. "Oh! Lady Bethany." He looked down at my basket. "I see you've been out."

"Yes." I paused. "How bad is it?"

He sighed heavily and rubbed his brow. "Bad enough, Lady Bethany. Bad enough."

I waited. "Could you expand on that?" I finally prompted him.

"We've lost a third of our men here. Thirty-thousand."

I frowned. "And the others?"

"Are hoping Darrell doesn't make an attempt on their cities."

Three days later, I went to the secret room. I had to see what was going on at home. I hadn't seen or heard from Erik since our confrontation in the palace. I was bored and lonely. The only thing I could think of that would help would be to see my Mom. Her face would be a comfort, even if I couldn't speak to her.

I smoothed my hand in front of the mirror and watched as it focused on my little brown house.

Mom didn't even know I was gone. She was on the phone with someone, talking and laughing intermittently. I sighed.

"She'll be fine," a quiet voice told me. Two hands pressed down on my shoulders.

"*She* will," I said, shaking my head sadly.

He sighed.

"Bethany...."

"Erik, I don't understand you. Don't you trust me?"

"Absolutely."

"Then why are you doing this?"

He paused for a minute. "It's best you don't know."

"I don't think so. To me, not knowing about stuff is a dangerous thing."

"You'll find out soon. Too soon for my liking." His tone made me more frightened than ever. I looked out the window. The moon was high in the sky and red as a ripe apple. I shivered.

"What are we going to do now?"

"We have to call in some men from the other cities. Ours are too far gone to do anything if we're attacked."

"But what if someone else is attacked?"

"Then they will have to figure it out. The palace is too important. If we fall, everyone falls."

I shrugged. I didn't know what to think anymore. It was all so confusing to me now. I didn't even know if it was worth it. It was almost as if what Eve had said was coming true. We were failing. Good creatures were dying for nothing.

Deep in my chest, the power was hibernating.

"Did we make an impact on him at all?"

"Yes. I don't think he'll be out like that again for some time. He's too vulnerable. We, at least, can count on our neighbors for support."

"Hmmm." I didn't know what else to say.

"The guard tells me someone paid you a visit."

I shuddered. "Yes."

"Do you want to talk about it?"

"No."

I WAS HAVING A HARD time finding Mia. The afternoon sun was hot and bright in my eyes, and everywhere I looked there was nothing but trees and flowers. I knew she had to be somewhere around here, because Arthur had told me she'd gone this way...or had it been the *other* way?

Uh-oh.

My talk with Erik last night hadn't exactly made me feel any better. I was still worried about the other fairies. And about him. And Mia and Leo. And myself, too, for that matter. It seemed like everywhere I turned, there was another problem waiting to be solved...or to kill us.

I stumbled on a rock and called out her name again. Where could she have gotten to? I stopped and stood, hands on my hips, eyes searching the forest. I really didn't think I'd gone the wrong way.

Then I heard something. A rustling in the leaves.

"Oh. Mia!"

Mia stood before me, evidently shocked to see me this far from the palace by myself. Leaves stuck out of her hair in every direction, and she had berry juice on the corner of her mouth.

"Lady Bethany...good afternoon."

I grinned. "I've been looking all over for you."

She looked me over carefully. "Why?"

"Aryan wants to look at you. He says you're stubborn as a cow and, if he has to, he's going to break into your room tonight so he can stitch you up."

Her eyes narrowed and her jaw moved slightly, chewing the berries. She brushed her hand against her lips.

"All right then," her voice was tranquil...sort of. "Let's go."

I left her at the door to the sickroom and headed towards the kitchen. It was filled with hungry soldiers. They all let me pass, but it was a long time before I could finally get the food I wanted because the kitchen was so backlogged. I was jealous—I bet Erik didn't have to deal with this.

As I waited for my food to come, I thought about my Mom. I wondered how she was again, though I knew she still hadn't noticed I was gone yet, probably.

It felt so weird...to be gone so long, and not have my mother try to call me once. Not that my phone worked here. It was perpetually left on my nightstand, unusable. But still....it felt odd to me. Unnatural. I wanted my mother.

I looked around. The room was filled with fairies that had been hurt in the battle. They gimped around on broken legs, had their arms up in casts...some even had eye patches. I felt a huge burst of sympathy explode in my chest and was thankful that none of my friends had suffered no such harm.

I ate outside, on the back porch. It was enclosed, but the walls were filled with windows, some of which were open because of the heat.

Erik was walking across the yard slowly. As he came closer, I saw a young fairy run up to him, bow low and start to speak. Her back was to me, and I couldn't see her face, but the way she motioned with her hands I guessed she had something she needed royal help with.

Erik's eyebrows crinkled up, and he shook his head. He said something, and she ran back. She didn't look happy. I frowned a little, wondering...He caught my eye and waved. I raised my hand.

Erik wanted to find Darrell. I knew it. But we were in no shape for any kind of battle—much less for a loss—we had to wait, even if waiting gave him a chance to escape.

And I didn't want to talk to Erik just yet.

I finished my meal quickly and went down to the hall of records. The hall was abandoned, lonely. I found myself moving carefully inside the old library out of respect for the silence. It was too still. It reminded me of a tomb. I picked out a couple of books and left hastily.

Jade met me as I went out.

"Why, Lady Bethany, I'm surprised to see you here!"

I resisted the urge to roll my eyes. Out of the corner of my eye, I caught sight of Erik again through the open window. He was coming towards us.

So much for avoiding him.

"Hello, Jade."

"Jade."

"Oh! Your Majesty. I'm sorry, I didn't see you there." Suddenly she looked frazzled, irritated. She turned back to me. "Well, I'll be seeing you, My Lady." She inclined her head towards us and hastened away.

"What was that about?" I inquired, frowning after her.

Erik looked just as puzzled. Then he grabbed my arm and led me out across the lawn. "We have to leave tomorrow."

"I'm coming."

"I know. I don't want you to, though."

My eyebrow twitched. "I don't care."

He sighed. Someone called him, then, surprising him. He kissed me on the head before turning to leave.

Once Erik was gone, I went to the secret room. I wanted to see my friends, but the only thing I could see in the glass was blackness and smoke. What could it possibly mean? I bit my lips, anxiety bleeding into my system anew.

Mia woke me up early the next day before the suns rose. I got up and dressed quickly. When I was ready, she led me out back.

I stopped short in the gravel walkway, surprised.

The army had been gathered. Erik sat on a white horse with a flowing mane, and a long horn jutting out of its forehead. At its side was another. He was black with a shiny red horn and long, long lashes. Though she seemed a little winded, Mia helped me up into the saddle; I grabbed hold of the reigns, looking to Erik for cues.

He smiled at me and checked over his shoulder. I noticed Leo was not of our number. I had not heard or seen anything of him since the last battle. I wondered how badly he had really been hurt.

The blood red moon shone overhead, casting an eerie glow over the bluish grass. The red glow gave the hooded heads of the soldiers around us a ghostly gleam. My breath caught as I took it all in. Someday I was going to have to ask Erik about the reason for this freakish occurrence.

But now was not the time. Erik clicked the reins on his horse, signaling commencement. We set out west, in the direction of the Lost Plains. Silence pervaded the group, but we made good time. By dawn, we had reached the Plains.

"You found where he's staying?" I asked.

Erik's expression twisted. "Not exactly. We're guessing at this point. Our spies we sent out to the City Arnek never came back. But the fae of the neighboring cities claim to have seen Darrell around quite a bit." He shifted in the saddle uncomfortably. "We're taking a chance, I know, but at this point I think it's the best we can do. We really don't have any other choices."

I nodded. "He's so evasive. It makes me nervous."

"You're lucky you didn't have to grow up with him," Erik replied, smirking grimly. His eyes were sad, and tired. I wished there was something that I could say that would comfort him.

"I suppose so."

We swept through the Plains and entered the small village after them. I recognized the town—and its bartender—immediately. She leaned against a small threshold, watching the procession with a broom in one hand. Her expression shocked me: it was so callous, so uncaring. It was almost as if she were watching a parade, rather than a military operation.

I scoffed. She pried her eyes away from the soldiers, then.

And saw me.

My back stiffened tightly at the malice that flooded her eyes. As if he knew what was going on, Erik's horse trotted up beside me, partially blocking her view.

The bartender disappeared into the doorway.

"She's an odd one," he murmured to me, his eyes on the threshold.

"Oh? I thought it was just me."

"No." We were silent for another moment. Then, "When we get there, I'm going to need you to lead a group around to the west side and charge. Can you do that?"

"You know I can." I looked up at his face. "Erik, it's going to be fine."

"I wish I could feel so positive."

The sun was high, almost directly overhead. I looked into the distance and saw a funny-looking orb in the sky, far to the right. I tapped Erik's arm and pointed. He grinned, slightly uplifted from his crummy mood.

"That's the sun."

"But"—

"I told you we have four," he reminded me patiently.

"Oh." I'd forgotten about that. "Wow." It was amazing—and strange—to see it from so far off, in such an odd position. It almost looked like it was setting. I gazed at it for a long time. And then something else caught my eye.

The large boundary stones that had once formed a barrier between the outside world and the town ahead of us lay in shambles. An enormous city was clearly visible through the cavernous holes. Large buildings rose into the sky, blocking the suns from view. I stared at the scene before me, feeling strangely disturbed for some reason I couldn't pinpoint.

Mia jerked the reins suddenly and drove her horse to the eastside. Erik gave the signal for me to take to the west. Obediently, I kicked my horse gently in the flanks. He dashed to the other side, and I noticed that some fairies stayed behind with Erik.

He was going to attack first. From the front entrance.

We ran through the thick forest for several miles. Then, as the city came back into view, I slowed, allowing some of my soldiers to take the lead.

Some of Darrell's men were ambling around mindlessly, almost drunkenly. Getting in, at least should be relatively easy. I looked back to my men.

"Ready?" I whispered.

The men in the brush nodded, hoisting their weapons, and steeling themselves for the fight.

I waited.

Heard the roar of the attack resound from the front gates.

Darrell's guards swung around and ran back towards the sound of the fight. They had their backs to us.

"*NOW!*"

We stormed after them. A small unit of twenty fairy soldiers ran ahead of me; they cut down the guards, clearing the way for the rest of us. We jumped over the three-foot wall fragments and rocks, tearing our way inside.

The sound of battle was deafening. I gave the reins a wild snap and we went full force into the center of town, where I knew Darrell would be keeping the prisoners.

The streets were a gory mess. I couldn't hear anything above the yelling and the sound of metal smashing against metal. My nose burnt with the scent of burning wood and hot steel.

I had to concentrate. "Look through the houses, find the others!" I screamed over the mayhem, watching as my men dispersed. I withdrew the dagger from a pocket in my uniform and hopped down. My horse whinnied and shied away from the noise.

"No, no," I murmured, brushing my hand over his muzzle. "C'mon." We went around to a large house, where the shadows were still deep enough to hide him. After that, I crept inside. It was empty. The next two houses were also vacant, and my men had as of yet found nothing.

I panicked. Could it be...But I wouldn't let myself consider the thought. We had to find the others. My horse was a little calmer, he let me lead him closer to the battle as we searched.

An explosion ripped through the atmosphere. The stone slabs under my feet shuddered, making me stumble. I grabbed hold of my horse's mane, but he was just as unsteady.

Something shattered around the corner. I froze, my hands tightened on the reins automatically.

Footsteps.

I was so terrified I could feel my heart beating in my palms. Every muscle in my body strained, waiting for the attack.

Three big fairies rushed at me. I managed to catch one under the chin with my fist, but my horse bucked. The movement knocked me to the ground.

Get up, get up.

I couldn't just yet. Adrenaline burned up in my veins; I was staring up into two of the most hideous faces I'd ever seen. I only had time to see the light reflecting from their knives.

And then they were gone.

The Colonel yanked me back onto my feet. "We need to get to the other men!"

Shocked at his rapid appearance, I shook my head, still catching my breath. "Not yet." Then I had an idea. "Cover for me!"

I ran through the streets, feeling the surge of power I always felt during a fight. I fought my way through to Erik, and stood behind him, guarding his back.

"Tell the men to stop rigging the buildings!"

"*WHAT*!"

"I said to tell the men to stop rigging the buildings!"

He kicked a man back, then turned to me. "We can't do that."

"You have to. The prisoners are all underground."

His expression changed into one of horror. But he nodded and spun to give the order.

A fairy with long black hair flew towards us out of nowhere. As I watched, he raised his elongated weapon to stab Erik in the back. I forced my body to move quickly. I caught the front of the weapon and snapped my arm back, sending both it and its owner flying through the air.

I didn't let the shock of what I'd just done slow me. I ran back through the streets, veering rapidly and going into the house that was the best bet. It was empty. I tried the next one.

Ugh! My brain throbbed. I had to find them before it was too late.

I opened the door at the back of the house, overjoyed to find the dank, spiraling staircase hidden behind the door.

"We will go down, Lady," the Colonel assured me, pushing me aside gently and starting down the stairs with the rest of my men with him. I waited impatiently.

Soldiers were running everywhere, fighting; fear touched me. What if we ran out of time? I turned back to the staircase, surely someone should be on their way back by now. I saw nothing.

"Genius," someone said behind me. I jumped. "Tell me, how long did it take you to realize they were here, my dear?"

I turned, shuddering. I knew who it was before I saw his face.

His face, so much like that of his brother. Only so twisted. So wicked. He smiled at me, and my body went cold. I drew my weapon slowly, keeping my eyes on his.

Darrell cocked his head to the side. "You know I've admired you for a long time, Bethany? You have strength. The kind I want in my army. But...." he played with his fingers idly. "*Unfortunately*, Erik beat me to you."

"Thankfully," I corrected him. My body was tense. I thought I heard the sound of armor clinking against the stone walls.

"Yes...I suppose you would think of it that way." He seemed to be deep in thought. "He never told you, did he? Who really has run of the Empire." He raised his eyebrows and motioned with his hands to the entire Kingdom.

"He didn't have to. I've seen enough," my voice was hard. Darrell's venomous eyes flashed.

"I'm not going to offer you anything, Bethany."

"I don't want anything from you."

"Are you sure?"

A breathless laugh escaped me. This displeased Darrell. He took a step forward. "You'll die..."

I backed up as he strode towards me. My hand inched for the overturned chair in the corner.

He saw that.

He was in my face instantly, knocking the chair away. His arm moved with impossible speed, but I ducked under his arm before he could touch me and brought the blade of my knife upwards, slicing him from his wrist to his fingertips.

He stared at the wound, shocked. As I watched him, the men reach the door. The Colonel was supporting a weak young girl, and there were many more behind him, pushing through the door to freedom.

Intending to order his capture, I nodded to the window.

He was gone.

The Colonel didn't notice my reaction. He was focused only on getting the fairies out safely. I helped him. Then I went back into the city to help Mia and Erik.

The battle endured for hours. I was glad—though in a very twisted, sick way—that Erik had brought the whole army. We wouldn't have been able to stand a chance any other way. As it was, I thought we were nigh on losing.

The suns had gone down, only a dim light covered the city. They left behind a graying, strange light. It hurt my eyes and made it hard for me to see what was going on. The others seemed to have no such problems.

Then came the last of the rebel's forces.

It very nearly killed me, without even touching me.

I saw the third wave of soldiers come in. I let my arm droop wearily and groaned. There were so many. It was like a cloud of feet and arms. Would this never end?

It came closer, I could see the faces. Human faces. Mixed with those of the fairies. I grimaced. I lifted my arm....

Too slow. Something hit me in the chest. I fell onto the hard ground. Something was pushing hard against my chest. I shoved it away and heard a body hit the ground. There was a grunt; I rolled onto my feet.

At the same time, another figure, slim and clothed in a long robe jumped up and snapped around. Her short hair ruffled in the breeze, and she stood, panting, ready to kill me.

"No." It couldn't be. It was impossible. "Marissa?"

She smiled grimly. That was the only sign of recognition. Her arm swept up, and I blocked the blurry movement, catching her wrists in my hands and throwing her to the ground.

"What's the matter with you?" I demanded. But something inside me already knew. It was Darrell. He'd gotten to her.

Suddenly, I wanted to kill him. I wanted to burn down the very forests that hid him and find him and destroy him the way he had destroyed so many others.

Marissa leaped up and smashed my in the face with a curled fist. I staggered back but retaliated with a football tackle. The orb in my chest was getting larger and larger by the second as she struggled with me. I rolled over and sat on her stomach, pinning her to the ground. Marissa lunged upward and cracked me on the forehead with her own.

My hands went up to my face automatically. Something hard hit me and then I was flying; my body hit a wall. The force of it made my head snap back, against the stones, and I fell, lifeless.

When I opened my eyes, Marissa was standing over me. She sneered, "You never could take a hit."

I groaned and struggled to get my hands under me. She waited. I stumbled forward but could do nothing. My whole world was spinning.

Not good, not good. Get up!

She had me by the throat. Marissa tossed me, like a rag doll, back into the wall. My head throbbed with pain and anger; my lungs burned. But more than anything else, the giant pulse I felt in my chest was beating, thumping, along with the rhythm of my heart, crushing my rib cage. I stood shakily, uncertain if I could hold myself up.

My hands and arms tingled. Marissa was waiting; she flexed her fingers and I realized with agony, that my best friend was having *fun*. I frowned, and she smiled, taking my pain for fear.

Regret coursed through me, before I even raised my hands. But the Empire and the fairies needed a king that would bring them life and hope. Darrell would never do that. And if Marissa was going to side with him, neither was she.

I curled my hands into fists, feeling the surge as the sphere bled outward. The sensation was amazing, it was pure power. I smacked my palms down onto the concrete slabs. A small jolt and then a feeling of brief release impacted in my chest.

The energy bubbled out, hitting the ground, and exploding. The ripples flowed through the city.

For the first time in a day, the city was silent. Marissa was on the ground. She looked up at me with eyes that were not her own.

So this was the secret Erik had been trying to hide from me. I stared at her for a long time before I could force myself to walk away. There was nothing I could do for her.

I saw several of our men on the ground and helped them up. We went together, to find our own and to take prisoners. Mia was the first general I came to.

She rubbed her neck and winced. "Next time you do that you might want to warn me."

I stopped. "How did you know that was me?"

"Erik told me your powers. It's why I convinced him to go down and get you." She picked up her weapon. "I think you killed your horse."

Erik was standing in the middle of what used to be the battlefield. I watched him long enough to see that he was okay, then went to find my horse.

He was all right, though the shock of the burst seemed to have dazed him. I led him back. I came across a little girl the men had missed, and picked her up, setting her on his back.

"What's his name?" she asked, momentarily distracted, but still blinking tears away.

I thought for a moment. "We'll call him Luna," I said.

She smiled, and my heart warmed. We watched as the men gathered and regrouped. I didn't see Darrell among the number of prisoners. Wonderful. Colonel Marc dragged Marissa from the ground. He shot me a grieved look; I dropped my eyes. My head hurt. I ripped the rubber band out of my hair, and let it fall around my shoulders. I was glad for that. It hid some of the horrid, savage scene from my eyes.

I led Luna and the girl who said her name was Eliza to the outskirts of town. Behind us the dreary army drudged. We were victorious. But only in the way that we'd won the fight. In the midst of it, we'd lost. We'd lost the lives of a thousand good men and many that, though they were not good, were looked upon as such by the many others that had loved them. No doubt we'd lost it all—brothers, sisters, fathers, sons...and friends. And not all because they had died in the battle, either.

There were some losses that were worse than death.

CHAPTER FIFTEEN

The camp was a little over a half mile from the city. None of us wanted to be too far away in case someone went back, but none of us wanted to be very close to it, either. We camped in a small area, each one taking comfort in the presence of the other. No one said anything, except for Eliza who, despite the horror of the day, seemed almost happy. She followed me around for the rest of the evening.

I couldn't sleep that night. I was thinking about Marissa and the other humans I'd seen in the battlefield today. Tears rolled out my eyes; I wondered what was going to happen to her now. Whether she hated me or not, I still loved her like a sister. Yet I knew there was no way of reversing...whatever it was Darrell had done to her. I sighed, and it caught in my chest. I pressed my lips together silently.

I don't know when or how I did it, but I eventually fell asleep. My dreams were haunted by colorful, terrific visions and the horror never lessened. When I woke up, the sun had already been up for a long time, and the soldiers looked like they were eating lunch. I sighed. Great.

I found Mia on the outside of camp, eating slowly. She offered a piece of her meal to me, and I took it and sat down beside her.

"Is, uh, is that what you two weren't telling me?"

"Which part?"

"Marissa."

She didn't answer, which I took for a yes. I dropped my head in my hands. "How long have you known?"

"A while. There's been a lot of trouble going on lately—you even sensed it before you left. She was lost to you and to us before you stepped foot into this world. We just hadn't known it."

"But how could that happen? Darrell was nowhere around her."

"He wasn't. His scout was."

My mind went blank. "Jason?"

Mia nodded, staring off into camp with dull eyes. "When someone moves through the Veil, they forfeit the laws of time completely. No matter how long you are away from there, you will always return to the point at which you left. We watched Jason cross through many times as a youngling. You just never noticed it because he always came back."

"What if he had never come back?"

"Oh, I think you'd have noticed that. But not for a long time."

I shook my head. I couldn't wrap my head around it, though it should make sense. All those times Jason harassed me to spend time with him, he was trying to recruit me. Silently, I said a thankful prayer that I never did as he asked.

"We only kept it from you because we wanted to protect you. Erik was trying to find a way to get them back."

I rubbed my arm anxiously. "I don't think there's anything we can do."

She didn't reply.

Eliza found me then and induced me to play a game of fairy patty-cake. It took her all of twenty minutes to teach me to play, and we played for hours. Arthur came over finally, smiling down on us.

"Well, you two look like you're having fun," he said, shooting me a skeptical glance. I looked down.

"We are," Eliza replied jovially.

He laughed. "Well, I'm glad." He bowed slightly. "My Lady, it's nearly time to leave."

I nodded and got to my feet. Eliza ran off, to join some other girls at their game, near the campfire. She stopped to wave at me as I passed.

I waved back and went on. The weight of the battle was crushing down on me now. Walking seemed to clear my head a little, but deep down I knew nothing would be okay again until Darrell was gone. I kicked at the clumps of dirt. The sharp, acrid scent of fire caught my attention and I walked down to the city.

I saw the smoke before I saw anything else. Flames engulfed the town, raging wrathfully. I stood and watched, strangely saddened by the spectacle.

"Come away from there, Bethany," Erik called to me, as though I were a child. I turned and shuffled over to him.

"How are you feeling?"

"Tired," I replied, looking at the grass and rubbing my grimy hand over my face.

"We'll be back soon."

I nodded.

"Bethany," his voice was softer now. I looked up at him. His almond blue eyes were worried. "I'm sorry..."

"Don't be. It's okay."

"No, it isn't."

I just kept looking up at him, pleadingly; though what I was pleading for, I had no idea. Erik seemed to understand. He hugged me tightly for a long minute, then led me back to the camp. We waited, while everyone got the things together and loaded it on the backs of the mules, always on guard for the next attack. Then we got on our horses and thundered out of that dark place, hopefully forever.

When we reached the smaller village, a loud cheer rose in the town. Someone even gave the king a large bouquet of strange sparkling flowers. I grinned halfheartedly, but other than that, I showed little interest in the festivities. My expression dampened some of the citizens gaiety, but I didn't care if I disappointed them. There was too much for me to process without pretending to be happy.

Erik didn't scold me for my unresponsiveness, but I sensed the anxiety radiating from him. I felt his eyes on my back often.

Upon finding that a doctor lived in the town, we opted to leave the sick with him, and most of the captives decided to stay as well. In the end, only ten continued on with us—little Eliza among them. She sat in front of me on the horse and waved to passersby. She, at least, seemed to be having a great old time of it. She looked up at me a few times, beaming, and for her I didn't have to force a smile.

Once outside the town, we picked up the pace. But the further we went, the worse I felt. My heart pounded lethargically in my chest, and worry agonized my mind. Maybe it was just an after effect of the battle, but I continuously looked over my shoulder now. Once, Erik caught my eye.

"He's coming. For me," I said. I knew it was true. I was more a target now than I had ever been. And I wasn't so sure this time he wouldn't kill me.

Erik nodded. He gazed off into the forest and slapped my horse on the rump so he would run faster. Eliza slumped in my arms and was soon too much for me to handle. When Erik reached his arms out for her, I let him take her.

We reached the palace at daybreak the next day, and, though I was nearly falling off my horse for exhaustion, I had to smile. Because I was home.

Leo met us at the door, and all my previous worries about him vanished. He was fine. He walked with a little bit of a limp, but his cheeks were as rosy as ever.

"Hullo, warriors!" he bellowed from the doorstep, opening his arms wide to embrace me and Eliza together. "Tales of your victory have proceeded you, my lucky lot."

Eliza giggled, and Leo ruffled her hair.

Erik was alighting his own horse. A valet took the majestic pearly beast's reigns and my own and led them to the stables.

Leo bowed low before Erik. "Sire."

"You look well, General."

Leo chortled. "I had ought to, Your Majesty, your cooks have kept a constant line of food coming to my door."

The first place I went with Mia was to the sick room, I wanted to talk to Aryan about my power. It felt weak in my chest, and I was worried. But Aryan was so preoccupied with the other patients that he didn't even have time to listen to me. I gave up. Maybe it was just because I was so tired.

Mia helped me back to my quarters and I fell into bed, letting delicious unconsciousness overpower me. I don't know how long I slept, but it felt like two seconds. Then I became rudely aware of a maid shaking my arm and shoving something purple in my face. I sighed.

"Fine."

About fifteen minutes later, I was clean and ready for the celebration feast. I followed the head maid Nikita to a room I had never been in before. It was brightly lit and decorated with thousands of fairy roses. The table was set primarily with silver, and some kind of creamy lace cloth covered it a hundred feet, from end to end.

I was shown the seat at one end of the table. At the other, I could just barely make out Erik's stately form, dressed in red and gold, wearing a crown on his head.

I wondered what had happened to Marissa, and felt a dull ache open up in my chest.

The meal soon chased away most of my worries, if not all of them. I had never seen so much food in all my life. And I couldn't eat all of what was placed in front of me, but that seemed to be all right with them. They always removed my plate and replaced it with another, brimming with food. Once, I thought I saw Erik laughing at my stuffed cheeks, but I couldn't be sure.

During the dessert, along with the food, the maids filled my glass with some strange bright purple liquid. I tasted it, and realized it was wine. Though, it wasn't ordinary wine; it was extremely sweet and very dry. I liked it enormously, however I forced myself to be moderate with it. I didn't want to make a spectacle of myself in front of some of the most important people in the kingdom.

I was bursting at the seams by the time dinner was over. I was glad I didn't have to get up right away; if I'd had to, I think I may have ended up rolling out the door I felt so heavy with food.

I spent a long time talking to Lady Kat and her husband, the shady Lord Covington. Lady Kat was a charming, talkative person, and I had a nice time talking with her. She never seemed out of interesting things to say. Lord Covington was quieter, and I felt for the most part he was watching me, as Leo had before. When he did speak it was some question about the battle. I answered them all as best I could but did not encourage him to keep on.

Finally, Lady Kat's bright green eyes registered my expression and she turned to her husband.

"Now, Covington," she scolded him with feigned joviality. "I don't think Lady Bethany appreciates being prodded about such things, dear."

"I was only asking."

"Yes, I know. But war isn't something to be made light of," she sounded as though she were scolding a child.

"How in kingdom, may I ask, did I make light of such a thing by asking a mere question?" he sputtered, out of breath halfway through, but refusing to inhale before his words were out.

I smiled at that, and heard the light, wafting music coming from the ballroom. Lady Kat giggled happily. "The ball is on!" She took her husband's arm and pulled him through the door. I followed behind quietly, picking a seat by the wall to rest as the rest of the guests filed into the center of the great room.

"Wouldn't My Lady prefer to dance?"

I grinned at his joking tone. "You know I don't know how. Besides, I'm too full."

He just smiled. "Come on….it won't kill you." He offered me his hand, and I sighed. I took it. Erik led me to the center of the floor.

Everyone moved to make way for their king with various small curtsies and bows.

I eyed him, raising an eyebrow and trying to look stern. "I'll warn you, Your Majesty, this is a dangerous undertaking."

"Oh, I'm sure I can handle it," he laughed.

It wasn't as difficult as I'd thought it'd be. Erik was patient, and, though I stumbled around clumsily at first, I was soon dancing along to the song like all the others were. I beamed, proud of myself.

Erik gave me a big smile. "You're in a better mood."

"How could I not be? It's so amazing here."

His eyes sparkled. "I thought you'd like it."

"Plus, I think it's the wine," I added, remembering the abrupt lift in spirits I had experienced by the time I'd finished the glass. We danced in silence for a little while, then when the song ended, he led me back to the chairs. I sat down, and he filled another glass and handed it to me. It wasn't wine, for which I was glad. I sipped it thirstily.

He sat down in the chair next to mine and gazed out at his subjects, they were twirling around on the floor and laughing. I smiled. Their enthusiasm and mirth was catching. Erik leaned back in his chair, more relaxed than I'd ever seen him.

He caught me watching him. "What?"

I bit back my smile. "Nothing. I just noticed you're not so tense anymore."

"It's the wine," he grinned. "Besides the fact, I'm savoring the victory."

"A well-deserved one."

"Mmm," he agreed. "Though I have to admit I doubt we would have won if not for your...talent."

I turned my eyes to the crowd, embarrassed. Lady Kat was dancing with Leo, giggling and prattling.

"Just who is she, exactly?"

"Lady Kat? She used to be the daughter of the mayor of one of the Lost cities. I forget his name. When Darrell took over, she lost her father, and came here to seek refuge. I couldn't turn her away of course, she had nowhere else to go. A few years later Covington came calling and they were married." He chuckled. "They don't always get along very well, but they're a pleasant couple nonetheless."

"She sure does talk a lot."

"More than anyone else in the Kingdom."

The Colonel ambled over. "Excuse me, Your Majesty, but if I may...." He held out his hand. I took it and we waltzed into the crowd. I sent a curious look over my shoulder. Erik was watching, looking a bit frustrated.

I turned my eyes to the Colonel. "I think you might just have some trouble for this."

"I might," he agreed. "But I wanted to speak to you, and King Erik doesn't always take news well."

"Oh, now don't tell me something if it's going to ruin my night, Colonel. We're having so much fun"—

"For now. I wanted to tell you that we caught Darrell"—

My heart leapt. "Really?"

"—visiting the prison. The girl slipped something through the bars to him. I don't know what it was and chances are she'd not going to tell us. We're interrogating her now, regardless."

"So, you *don't* have him?" I asked, confused.

"No. I thought My Lady should know."

I nodded, dropping my arms as the music stopped. I looked down. "Thank you, Colonel."

"I apologize, Madame."

I tried to smile. "Don't. You did nothing wrong."

I returned to Erik then, and whispered the story into his ear. He rose from is chair. "Did Colonel say which way he went?"

"No, and I don't think you'll be able to find him this time of night, anyway."

"She won't talk."

A sharp pang pierced my heart. Erik studied my face solemnly. He sat back down and rubbed his face.

"Bethany, I'm going to ask you to do something you're not going to want to do, but you'll have to."

"I'll question her," I said, before he could ask.

"Thank you."

I rose off my chair and started for the door. He caught my arm. "Not yet, stay a while. The party isn't over yet—she'll still be there in the morning, I'm sure."

I plunked back down on the chair and leaned against his arm. "I'm tired of all this betrayal and death," I complained. He rubbed my shoulder, eyes on the unsuspecting crowd.

"We all are. Don't worry. It'll be over soon."

"How can you know that?"

"I just do. It won't be much longer, and things will go back to normal."

I sighed.

"You-hoo....! Your Majesty—Your Highness!" We looked over to see the bartender girl. Victoria. I laughed.

"How on earth did she get in here?"

"I don't know," Erik sounded amused.

Victoria stomped over, swaying widely from side to side. She nearly fell, grabbed the table for support, tripped on her shoes, caught herself, and finally, stood before us. Her feathery pink had sat up on her forehead in front of her eyes. She blew air and shoved it back, looking down at us with wild eyes.

I hid my face in Erik's shoulder, trying to hide my laughter. He forced a smile down and faced her, pinching my side. I sat up obediently and looked her full force in the face. It was so hard not to laugh.

She swayed a little bit, and suddenly dipped down into a messy curtsy.

"I'm surprised," she told me, voice slurring. "You did well for a human—strangely dignified for your kind—uhuh—weird." She gave Erik a dark look. "Not...to say...I aprooooove. Because I don't." She closed her eyes, shaking her head languidly. She tipped backwards, then somehow managed to catch herself and stood up straighter. She gave me a thumbs up. "Goodluck!" Victoria stumbled away then, still staggering, looking green.

We burst into laughter. I caught sight of Mia and another fairy, giggling behind their hands. She caught my eye and we both laughed outright. Victoria disappeared through the door, and two guards hurried after her.

"I think she's running across the yard."

Erik didn't answer, he was laughing too hard to speak.

The guests danced on, oblivious to the scene. We danced again, and after the ball, Erik walked me back to my quarters. I noticed the torches had been lit. There was no moon.

It wasn't till later that night that the realization hit me. Painfully. I'd been betrayed. I tossed under the silken sheets and whimpered, tears sprinkling down on the pillows, one after another.

What could possibly have happened? Marissa was supposed to be my best friend. Unable to lay in bed any longer, I got up and went to the long sofa near the window. I sat there, staring out at the dark scene before me, thinking about all the years Marissa and I had been friends.

Well she's not anymore, a little voice in my head snapped. *Get over it.* My body shook with sobs; I wanted to go home. To wake up and find that this has all just been another nightmare.

Erik's words from before reverberated in my ears. "We can't send her back—it's too dangerous. And if we release her...she might very well try to kill you. The council wants an execution. An example for all those who conspire against the empire."

The tears had welled up into my eyes at that. Despite what she had done, I didn't want Marissa to die. But Erik had continued quickly. "I'm trying to convince them otherwise. We don't know exactly what it is Jason did to her. It's possible it can be reversed. In either case, the best we can hope for her is a life sentence."

A life sentence was better than death. "Thank you."

"You don't have to thank me, Bethany. It's the right thing to do, all things considered."

AS SOON AS IT WAS LIGHT enough, I got out of bed; I wanted to get the interrogation done with as soon as possible. My heart weighed heavily inside me as I dressed and combed my hair. Mia gave me a sympathetic look in the hall when I went by; I tried not to let her see how upset I was getting, but I think she saw through my act.

I was led to the prison by an old general. I shuffled my feet reluctantly as we entered a cold, bare stone room. He left me there to get Marissa. I sat down in a chair, steeling myself for the process to come. It was all I could do not to get up and run back out the door. The orb in my chest throbbed weakly.

The door opened with a scraping, squeaking sound. I looked up, and Marissa appeared through the doorway. Surprise lit her eyes, followed by dismay, and then something else. Something I didn't want to see. She leaned up against the wall as the guard closed the door and glared at me in silence.

"What did you do?" My voice was hard. It surprised her.

"Nothing."

"Don't lie to me Marissa. You're just going to make it worse for yourself. I'll help you as much as I can—"she scoffed—"but you have to start talking."

"I don't want your help."

"You will. You're not going to get home without it."

She shot me a look.

"The Veil's been closed. No one can go in or out. Not without my okay."

Marissa glowered at me, eyes narrowed. I sat back in my chair and waited for the news to sink in. She'd break. Marissa wouldn't want to stay here forever.

But she shook her head and smirked. "You won't help me. You never even tried."

"I didn't really get a chance, M., you were trying to kill me, remember?"

"I'm talking about Jason. You knew what he was up to. You knew what he was doing. You never said a word."

"I tried to warn you, Marissa." She snorted. I snapped up out of the chair. "I want to know what you gave Darrell."

"Nothing, I said that already."

"You're lying."

"Oh? And you're going to do what?"

I scowled, angry now. My chest throbbed. I stalked past her. She watched me go.

"Well? What?"

"I'm going to leave you here. I don't need you. I can just find Darrell and throw him in here, like you. Right beside your cell." I shrugged. "Problem solved. I just thought I'd make things easier for you by giving you a chance."

And with that, I walked out. I spotted the Colonel at the door.

"Get the horses ready. We're going hunting." I tried to sound brave, but the truth of the matter was that I was afraid, for the first time. I felt the power shivering inside of me.

He told me that it was going to take a couple of hours before anyone was up and ready, and I remembered suddenly how early it was. I sighed and nodded.

Eve caught up to me on the way out. I wasn't in the mood for discussion, but she didn't seem to notice.

She was going to town and wanted to know if I'd come along. I remembered the visit I'd been planning and nodded glumly. We walked towards town, Eve chattering all the way.

"But you know, I really don't think it's worth it."

"What's not worth it?" I asked. I suddenly felt very tired, and my power was still shaking. Maybe I should stop now and go see Aryan.

Eve raised her arms and dropped them, her hands slapping against her thighs. "Everything! This war...we're going to lose it."

"I don't believe that," I said quietly.

"Of course, you don't! You know, that's why you're here. Personally...if it were me, I wouldn't have come." She shook her head and sniffed. I exhaled in a loud puff.

Thankfully, we had made it to Nina's door. I said goodbye.

"You're not going to walk back with me?"

I shook my head. "I might be a while, Eve, I want to see how she's doing and stuff."

"Oh. All right. Buh-bye!"

I escaped inside. Nina was at the table, eating breakfast when I came in.

"Hi, Nina."

"Ooof!" She scrambled up out of her chair, stumbled, then finally, she curtsied. I tried not to laugh.

"Lady Bethany, I wasn't expecting you."

I waved a hand. "Oh, don't worry. I just wanted to see how you're doing, that's all."

Her eyes softened. "I'm doing very well, My Lady, thank you. Are you hungry?"

I had breakfast with her, even though I'd already eaten I was still starving. When we were finished, I told her goodbye, and let her know that, should she need anything, she could count on me for it, and then I left.

I met Leo and Mia on the palace grounds. They'd been waiting for me to return, and I saw that, in addition to their two horses they also had an extra one, and Luna. I smiled and climbed up on Luna's back.

CHAPTER SIXTEEN

We rode our horses out into the forest. Abruptly, Luna stopped, he lifted his nose, sniffing the air.

Leo caught up to us, paused at my side.

"What?"

"I don't know. Something's here," I answered, watching Luna's reaction. He snickered and tried to go back; I kicked his flank gently. "No, Luna. All right, Leo. You go right, Mia go left, I'll take the path."

I nudged Luna gently, and he started forward again, walking slowly. Fear radiated from him. I patted his neck. We glided through the brush and trees slowly. My eyes roved everywhere, trying to see everything at once. Nothing moved. No sound was made. Yet Luna was certain there was danger ahead. My heart fluttered.

He pulled back again, and I jerked the reigns. "No!" I hissed.

A twig snapped under his hoof and made me jump slightly. A light breeze wafted past us, carrying leaves along with it and dropping them in the roadway.

As we went on, it got harder for me to breathe. It was like before when I could feel the menacing presence riding behind my back. I looked over my shoulder but saw nothing.

Something blasted by the trail.

Luna whinnied loudly, rearing up on his hind legs. And then I was air born. I flew back, hitting my head on a tree trunk, and fell to the ground. I watched tumultuously as Luna galloped off, leaving me behind. My vision swirled; I shook my head. The leaves rustled. I snapped around, frightened. The orb throbbed in my chest. I got to my feet and stood, gazing through the forest.

The leaves rustled once more, behind me now. I spun, backing into the trail. "Who's there?"

No one answered.

I released the weak energy from my chest and felt it radiate down my arms, to my fingertips. They twitched.

Then I heard it. Something coming, fast.

Without thinking, I planted my hands to the ground and let go of the power inside me. It erupted silently, flinging my hair back and shaking the trees.

I waited. Heard nothing.

Then, "Bethany….!"

Whoops. "Sorry, Mia!"

She appeared, leading her strawberry stallion. She pressed her hand to her head. "What's going on over here? I think Leo just flew into the lake."

"There's someone hanging around here. It spooked Luna."

I pointed in the direction my horse had gone, Mia followed my finger with her eyes and sighed. "Well, let's try to find them, then."

Leo came from somewhere in the trees. "Wow! That was cool."

He sounded like a teenager. I laughed.

"Bethany says we have company." Mia told him without looking at him.

He nodded. "I know. I heard him, moving around just before Lady Bethany blew me off my horse."

"Sorry." I grinned apologetically. Leo winked at me and nodded.

We searched the area; I was starting to give up hope when we spent close to an hour without anything to show for it. Then I heard a something running. I called out, and, so soon, Leo was there, standing over a scrawny-looking man in a t-shirt and jeans. He stared up at us dazedly.

"So, you're behind all this hide-and-seek, hmm?"

The man blinked, and the power in my chest fizzled out. I clenched my fists. I turned to Leo. "Get him up."

Leo tied his hands together and thrust him on the spare horse, while Mia went to find Luna. She brought him back several minutes later. He waved his great dark head at me in apology. I rubbed his forehead.

I was disappointed. Sure, we got a prisoner, but I'd been hoping to catch Darrell, not this punk. I had a sense that Leo was chagrined as well. We went back home and handed the boy off to the guards.

I was sitting in the porch, munching on sweets and sipping tea, when Erik came up. "Congratulations."

I made a face. "I was holding out for Darrell."

Erik snickered. "He's slippery. We'll probably make it all the way to the end of the war before we get our hands on him."

"I don't think my patience will last that long, to tell you the truth."

"It'll be fine," he reassured me.

I didn't reply, playing with the ruffles on my dress.

"Besides, I think you need a break from the war anyway."

"Is that possible?"

"Yes, of course it is."

I turned to look on him. I was about to ask him what he had in mind when something occurred to me. "Can't we use the mirror to see where he is?"

He looked surprised. "I've tried. Wherever he is, the mirror won't show it."

"How come?"

He thought for a moment. "I think it's him. Usually the mirror will show whoever one wants to see. There's a part of him that makes the mirror go black. It can't see through who he is to see what he is." He looked down at me, "You understand?"

I nodded. I popped another treat into my mouth and put my feet on the bench. "I just wish we could catch him, that's all."

"You have to be careful, Bethany." I looked up, and he was staring out into the forest. "Because all he wants right now is to catch *you*."

"I know. He tried to convince me to join him the day of the battle." I shook my head. "I could've had him then, but I didn't move fast enough."

He didn't like that. His back stiffened, and his azure eyes returned to mine. "Why didn't you tell me this before?"

"It didn't seem important."

Erik exhaled loudly. I got to my feet and trotted off the porch into the bright sun. He walked beside me, frustrated. I ignored him and went to the secret room.

"What are you doing?"

"Trying something." I tried to see my mother, and Tracy, and—as usual—I could. I went ahead and tried Marissa, and felt a horrid, jagged pang when I couldn't. Neither could I see Jason or Tanya. Erik waited behind me impatiently. I tried one more. Victoria. Instantly, the mirror showed me her, gossiping with her customers at the bar.

I smiled, and, on a hunch, tried to see Daniel's friend. It worked. He was talking to someone rapidly. "Bingo," I murmured. Erik stepped forward.

"Who is that?"

"That's the man that told Daniel to kill me." I pointed to the blackness to the right of the mirror; the part the fairy was arguing with. "And I'd bet an eye, that's your brother."

Erik grimaced at the connection, then took a step closer, he looked into the glass. "Now if only we could see where that is..." He pushed me out of the way gently and maneuvered the mirror so we could see the outside of a tiny shack.

"That's not too far from here." He glanced at me. "I passed it on a walk the other day. It's about a mile northeast of here, through the forest." He nodded and dropped his hands.

"Do you want me to go get the men?"

He shook his head. "Not yet."

"Why not?" I demanded. "It's perfect!"

"Bethany. The men are tired. They're hurt. Give it another day or two, okay?"

I sighed. He was right. I hadn't seen anything of our men the past couple of days. "All right. But what if he gets away?"

"He won't." We went out then, as Eliza ran into the room.

"Bethany!" I swung her up onto my hip, and Erik locked the door. She hugged me. "Can I ride Luna, pleeeeeaaaase?"

I smiled. "Sure. Go get your riding clothes on." I set her down and she ran off. I turned to Erik. "Let me know when things change, okay?"

"I will." He sighed.

"What?"

"Nothing, just frazzled, that's all."

"What do you have going on today?"

"I have to go down and see what we can do about the city we burnt down. The citizens want it built back up, though I don't know why on earth they would...I have a few more meetings to go to than I'd like. And then there's a border dispute between the Auyen Cities I have to take care of." He sighed again wearily. I frowned.

"Sounds like you should take a breather."

"I can't. Nothing would incite the people against me more than if I ignored their problems."

"Yet you can be expected to do everything? That doesn't sound right to me." We were walking towards the stables, taking our time.

"Come ride with us."

"Bethany, I would if I could, but I just told you"—

"Yeah, yeah, I know. Fate of the world rests on your shoulders." I grabbed his hand anyway and tugged him to the stables where Eliza was waiting.

She curtsied politely and looked at me with huge eyes. "You have to leave again?"

"Nope." I grinned and motioned over my shoulder at Erik slyly. "King Erik is coming with us for once."

Eliza's eyes widened. "Cool."

I hopped up on Luna's back and pulled her up behind me. "Come on, Your *Majesty*," I teased him. "We don't have all day."

"Pleeeese?"

Erik's sour expression softened; he sighed. "All right, then." He climbed onto the back of his polished white mare, and we were off. I took the rough trail. Eliza bounced up and down and giggled as Luna galloped through the forest, leaping over logs and boulders along the way. We could hear Erik close behind us. I felt Eliza lean away from me as she looked over her shoulder, then she turned back to me. "Faster, faster!"

I grinned and kicked Luna's flanks. He started forward with a jolt, soon the trees were racing past us, the colors blurring in the background. We ran through the high grass and the underbrush. Luna jumped over logs and big rocks like they were nothing. We broke out of the forest line within a matter of seconds and kept going. The high grass whipped my ankles and caught at my shoes. I turned a bit, laughing.

Erik was coming up close behind us. He was laughing, too. Moonshine was running faster, and within seconds he had almost caught us.

We squealed, and I forced Luna to go faster. I could hear his heavy breathing as we tore through the valley, and up over a large hill. When we had outdistanced King Erik a bit, I allowed Luna a break, and we trotted up the hill.

By now we'd reached another valley, one I had never seen before. I veered to the right, and we blazed through it. I could hear Eliza's breathless laughter in my ears. We took to the hills and stopped, still laughing.

I turned Luna around.

Erik wasn't there. Eliza and I looked at each other and giggled.

"I hope he's not lost," Eliza said. I was too breathless to reply.

We waited, and soon we saw the mare's white head bobbing up and down, coming up the hill. I felt Eliza squeeze my stomach.

"Go, go, go, go, GO!" She squealed.

I bit my lip, and pulled the reins sideways, towards the mountains. We ran up to them, checking every so often behind us, but after I while I thought he'd given up. I marched Luna up into the mountains. The way was slippery, covered with tiny stones that rolled under his hooves when we passed. He slipped backwards a couple of times, but I nudged him, and he got up it anyway.

I spotted Erik out of the corner of my eye, coming up over the hills. I nudged Eliza and pointed, she grinned. Her cheeks were red from the ride. Probably, mine were too. I clicked my tongue at Luna, and he turned away from the edge unwillingly.

We followed the winding trail up the mountain, stopping every few seconds to tease Erik, who hadn't yet made it to the base of the mountain. We waved and continued on our way. We reached boulders now, sturdier ground for Luna, but just as dangerous; I slowed him to a gentle trot. We made our way up, up, up the mountain path. Once I thought I heard Erik's horse Moonshine coming up behind us, but the sound faded away.

"What was that, Lady Bethany?"

"A deer, I think."

But then the deer reappeared. We could hear it passing us, from the higher cliff. I reigned in Luna and we scanned the rocks.

"I don't see it."

"Me neither." We shrugged, and I nudged Luna to go on. The trail was just flat enough now that I could get him to running again. I kicked his sides and we took off. Eliza screamed. It was a different kind of scream. I jumped and looked back to make sure she was all right. I followed her shaking finger to the rocks. Something large and brown disappeared behind the rocks. Seconds later, he came out, running down across the trail and into the trees. A man, I thought a first. A very hairy shirtless man with mussed up long brown hair and a beard. There was a horse following.

But by the time he made it to the center of the trail, I realized it was no horse following behind him. He was half and half.

A centaur.

Luna screamed, he reared up on his legs for the second time, and we both fell off.

The momentum of my fall sent me rolling. I was too stunned to notice much, except when the ground ran out underneath me, my heart bailed out, too. A bloodcurdling scream tore through my throat, and I grabbed wildly for something, anything, to hang on to.

A thick brown hand reached out and caught my wrist. I hung there, suspended between the heavens and the hard rocks below. I could see the centaur at the bottom, looking up at my terror-struck figure, cocking his head to the side. Mystified.

I looked up then. My jaw dropped, and a new kind of fear swept over me icily.

It was Darrell.

I stared up at him, not sure whether to be grateful and wait till he got me over the edge to push him off, or to just tell him to let me go.

Before I had the time to say anything, he pulled me over the rough lip of the mountain. I couldn't see Eliza. I didn't have time to look for her. He yanked me off my knees.

"You're mine now," he told me. I struggled hard, but he wouldn't let me go. The power in my heart throbbed weakly.

That disturbed me. Why was it so weak?

I tried to use it and succeeded in freeing my arm. Yet when I turned to fly, he grabbed my waist and hauled me back to the horse. I didn't stop fighting, but the power was all used up, and it wasn't going to help me, anyway.

"Do you honestly think I'm going to fight for *you*?" I demanded through my teeth. "Huh?" I clawed at his hand, trying to push him away.

Darrell jerked me closer and hissed menacingly. "No! I think you're going to be the perfect bait for our dear king. Funny I never thought of that before, isn't it darling?" He wound a thick leather rope around my wrists and flung me over the butt of his horse, he set off at a fast gallop, down the mountain.

I bounced sickeningly as we went. We were going much too fast, or I would have tried to roll off the horse.

We took an alternate route down the mountain—Erik should be coming up the opposite side. I hoped he'd found Eliza. Darrell slapped his chestnut mare hard on the side once we hit the base of the mountain. And I lost all hope. The earth was speeding by in flashes of green and brown, melted together. I closed my eyes and let my head drop against the saddle.

The galloping motion of Darrell's horse made everything worse. I squeezed my eyes shut, trying to calm down. *It's going to be okay*, I told myself. *It's going to be okay. Erik will come for me soon.* My power, like the last glowing ember of a wildfire, throbbed weakly. Its feeble strength made me hope, while it also made me want to give up.

After about half an hour, I heard the roar of a crowd, I lifted my head to see several hundred dirty, fat soldiers, and some fairies—just as dirty—cheering insanely. Darrell slowed the horse to a prance that took us through the meadow to the shack I'd seen in the mirror. I felt some relief. At least Erik would know where to come looking for me.

Darrell jumped off the horse, grabbed me up with some difficulty. I kicked him in the face several times before he was able to sling me over his shoulder. He lugged my inside.

No one was in the little cabin; Darrell dragged my still struggling form to the back of the house. He opened the door, ripped off the leather rope from my wrists, and shoved me through. I tumbled down the stairs, landing at the bottom.

A horrible snapping sound came from my arm. Pain shot up my arm and through my shoulder. I held it close to my chest, groaning in pain. I rolled over onto my feet. The door slammed shut, cutting off what little light I'd had.

I restrained a sob, as I finally realized I was all alone in the darkness. The faint throbbing in my chest was building now, but it was nowhere strong enough to be of any use to me yet.

I felt along my arm and shoulder and winced. It was broken in at least two places. I pounded the ground with my hand. A frustrated grunt escaped my throat.

Wonderful, I thought. *Just great.* I slumped against the wall, and waited, half in a daze, for whatever was about to happen next. Hours later, I heard someone run into the cabin. They opened the door, and I was suddenly wrenched up and pushed outside. It took a moment for my eyes to get used to the light.

When they did, I was surrounded by soldiers. They glared at me in unfriendly ways; each of them carried a weapon of some sort. I stared back at them, refusing to let them see the sudden terror that I felt. I looked away from their cruel, horrid eyes, towards the meadow. My breath caught.

Erik.

And the army behind him.

My gloomy expression broke into a smile. He waved once, and I did so as well, finding it hard, because my hands were tied again and the pain in my right arm was excruciating. The sight of his graceful white horse sent my heart a-flutter.

I was going home! Back to my quarters with all the other ladies, and, hopefully, I'd find Aryan somewhere.

But my hope wasn't to last long. The soldiers formed a wall in front of me, separating me from him.

"No!"

Darrell rode into view. I glowered at his back spitefully as he went to the middle of the little field.

Erik spurred his horse, to meet him. I tensed, watching the scene play out slowly. My heart thumped forcefully, and with fear and hope. I hated watching this.

I continued to watch as they talked. It started out calmly, and then, when Darrell motioned back to the camp—to me, I guessed—Erik clenched his hand around the reins. He said something, and Darrell shook his head. I could see his smile and felt a rush of hatred for this man.

I could only imagine what Darrell was saying. My hands clenched, and I pressed my lips together, shooting a look at the soldiers. One glared back at me and raised his axe menacingly. Instantly I dropped my eyes, then looked back to the twosome in the meadow.

Erik was motioning to me violently and pointing at his brother's chest. Darrell knocked his hand away and responded with a rant of his own. Moonshine took a couple steps back and to the side, and I tensed, waiting for Erik to snap.

But he didn't. He said something to Darrell in a low tone, then turned and went back. My eyes narrowed.

"Looks like you're not worth it," a fat man jeered at me. I ignored him. I watched as the army drew back.

Erik spoke a few words to Mia. She listened, then snapped her head around, glaring. She argued with him for a few minutes, but he eventually won her over. By order, I assumed, from Erik's stern expression when he spoke to her. She slunk back. I felt a twinge of the power in my heart, and wished Aryan were here.

CHAPTER SEVENTEEN

Erik had been gone a while; I was starting to doubt he'd come back for me after all. Darrell seemed to think he'd won the war. He went on and on about sacred traditions and the inevitable "power of the first born," all day long. Had I been paying any attention; I would have thought the man had lost his mind. But I was too busy feeling sorry for myself. I sat on an old log and fidgeted with a long piece of straw as I sulked.

Darrell's camp was a dirty thing. Nothing like the put-together camps my men made up. Just thinking of how well my fairies had presented themselves in war made me feel a surge of pride for them, and a new kind of hatred for the sloth of my enemies. Didn't they ever bathe?

Darrell's men were worse than dirty, wearing rags and long beards; putrid odors followed them whenever they passed by me. Some seemed to be perpetually drunk, and others never moved for anything other than to eat or for bathroom breaks. I couldn't count the number the times I'd heard them belching or passing gas.

I kept to my log, as far from the main group as they would allow.

Once, Darrell came to sit beside me. I tried to snub him at first, but he didn't show any intention of leaving.

"What do you want?" I snapped finally, running my fingers through my hair anxiously.

"Bethany, you have to come fight beside me. I can't imagine what the Kingdom would be like without you to help me lead it," he sounded like he was doing his best to sound pitiful for me.

I rolled my eyes. "I've read the histories; I know who you are and what you've done."

He was quiet for a minute, watching the brawl that was taking place at the edge of camp.

"The histories are biased," he said at last.

I didn't say anything.

"You don't know me," he finally murmured.

Anger boiled hot in my chest. I thought of everything he had done to me, to Erik, and even Marissa. And I snapped. Before I really knew what I was doing, I was screaming names at him, accusing him and his men of every crime I could think of. His eyes flashed as he listened to me rant, nostrils flaring. I didn't care. I spit on his face.

He slapped me.

All the noise stopped. They stared. I picked myself up with one hand, and stood before him, feeling the same kind of rage as I had the day he'd attacked Erik and me in the meadow at my home.

Only this time I didn't know what to do. My strength was failing, my arm broken, I was alone and surrounded by hostile faces, one of which had just beaten me. Already I could feel the blood rushing to that spot on my cheek, turning it bright red. My face tightened.

"Erik will kill you for that." I snarled at him between my teeth.

"He didn't even try to save you, girl. I wouldn't count on it."

"That's a lie. And a mistake." I was still facing him, standing still. I turned slowly, eyeing the slobs that surrounded me. "All of you have made a mistake."

Their faces wore various expressions of fury, but I pretended not to see that. I moved away from Darrell and sat down at the base of a large tree...I played with the dust, drawing pictures in it so I wouldn't have to look up into their eyes. I knew what I'd see there, and I'd seen enough of it already.

I could feel Darrell's eyes on me, even though I never looked at him. He didn't leave.

"You've got heart, girl. I'll give you that."

I ignored him.

"It was a mistake to wait so long. I should never have let Erik get to you."

"Even if you'd brought me through the Veil first, I would never have taken your side."

He didn't reply. He stood up, threw his can of food to the ground, kicked it into the fire, and walked away. I listened to his tantrum, smiling to myself. When he was gone, I heard the men start to move again. They grumbled under their breath and shot me dark looks. They didn't look worried, only puzzled and livid.

I went down to the basement willingly that day, relieved to be away from them all. My shoulder ached and burned. I readjusted it several times as I tried to sleep against the cold hard stone floor but moving only made it worse. So, I just lay there, waiting for sleep to come, trying to ignore the vicious pain.

I don't know how long I was down there, it felt like years. And then one day someone came down to get me.

It wasn't quite daylight yet, and I was hoping that it was an escape, but then I saw the dark, motionless form nearby and all my hopes vanished.

Darrell was there, waiting, watching the red moon go down. The soldier at my side announced my presence, then left. I noticed Darrell was the only fairy about, and none of the humans had gotten up yet, either. I watched him warily. The orb in my chest throbbed slightly.

He turned to me. The glow of the fading moon reflected off his handsome face, giving it and eerie look. I shrank back unconsciously.

"I'm sorry. I was far too bold the other day. I didn't think that the men were so repulsive to you, and that that might affect the way to see *me*." He smiled. "I'm so used to being with them, I don't notice anymore. Maybe that'll be something you change."

I didn't reply.

"But, now that we're alone. I'd like to repeat my offer. Bethany, we can win the war without you. But it would be so much easier if you'd help me."

I narrowed my eyes.

"I thought I told you no already."

"You have," he sighed. "But I really don't want to go through the trouble of killing you, darling. It's too messy, and you're far too important to me—and the cause—to meet your end in that way."

I just looked at him, letting the bleakness in my expression speak for me. I didn't think I could trust myself to talk to him, without getting slapped again.

He sighed. "Bethany, you don't know what you're doing. You're helping him destroy the Empire."

"I'm helping him *save* it."

"No."

"Oh. Yes. Yes, Darrell. You're the one that's trying to destroy it."

He looked at me, his face without expression.

I went on. "You had a chance to get the throne, anyway. And you threw it away, remember?" His face fell, as I reminded of his error. "Do you think she would appreciate this?"

"Rachelle died. Very long ago," he told me in a quiet voice. The pain in it was evident, but I felt no sorrow for him.

"Don't expect me to replace her for you, because I won't."

Anger flashed across his face; his jaw tensed "Fine then." He waved me away. "Have it your way."

I wasn't allowed to eat anything at all that day. I could tell Darrell was hoping I was just soft enough that that would change my mind. But I had more pressing cares on my mind than food. When he called me back to him, and my answer had not changed, he ordered me to be thrown back into the cellar.

I spent the whole next day there, in the basement, wondering where Erik was and when he was coming for me. He had to be soon.

"Hurry," I moaned one night. I'd argued with Darrell again and, as always, my rash tongue had gotten me into trouble. I felt awful, certain that he was watching, and that he was angry, and hurt, seeing me suffer.

But I knew, too, that the only way Darrell was going to let me go was if either he died, or Erik gave up the Kingdom. The men were beat, they were tired. They couldn't fight, and Mia wouldn't let him give himself over to Darrell—for which I was grateful.

I felt the orb growing day by day. I stored it all in the massive bubble I felt pulsating through my heart, reserving it for when I would escape.

The door screamed open, and I raised my head. I couldn't see his face, but knew it was one of Darrell's men. He dropped my supper down on the stair in front of me, turned, and lumbered away.

I groaned. Pushed the food away. It smelled horrible. I wrapped my arms around my sore middle and tried to sleep. My arm was numb, now. But it had been bothering me all day. The sudden lack of feeling made me worry.

I wasn't allowed out of the cellar at all the next day. Darrell must have given up on me. Now, I was going to stay here until someone came to get me...or I died...in which case I would probably be here forever.

I shuddered and my stomach turned at the thought. I lay against the cool floor and curled up into a ball on my good side. That helped a little; I pressed my hands under my chin and tried to take a deep breath. It hurt. Had my ribs been broken, too?

I heard arguing outside. I listened hard. It sounded like someone was trying to desert. I could hear Darrell's loud voice ordering him back to his tent. This the soldier refused to do, and a roar broke out among the soldiers. I tensed, waiting for the moment when he would join me at the foot of the stairs. But he never did. And I relaxed.

I was awakened again by the sound of clashing metal. I lay there for a moment, dazed. I didn't believe what I was hearing.

But the sound of the battle did not go away, and I made myself get up. I stumbled and leaned against the door. I wondered if I could use the energy to get up the stairs. I focused...got one foot up the stair...

The door blew backwards, and a man stepped through. I froze, unable to see his face at first. I watched as he turned towards the light, his slanting blue eyes searching frantically for something in the darkness.

My heart skipped a beat, and hope rushed over me for the first time in days. I beamed, though the pain made it hard to breathe.

"Erik!"

Erik exhaled, relieved. "What on earth were you thinking?" he demanded, picking me up.

"I didn't know he'd be there."

"Obviously. Next time don't try to outrun me, okay?"

"'Kay."

He raced me up the stairs. The noise got worse, the closer we came to the battlefield. I rested my head against his chest tiredly. The wind caressed my face. We left the house....and then stopped.

It was Darrell. He stood before us, weapon in hand.

"Get out of the way, Darrell," Erik snapped, his voice low and menacing.

Darrell started to speak, but I quickly raised my hand, and let go of all the power that had been building up in me since my kidnapping. Darrell flew back, and everyone else went down like dead bats. Erik rocked backwards. He swayed a bit, then stepped back with one foot to catch himself. He looked down at my face, surprised.

I looked up at him, smug, my muscles hurting. "I owed him that one."

"I know." Suddenly his face was livid.

Erik rushed me back to the sick chamber and left me with Aryan. I lay still while he worked on me, bandaging my legs and setting my arm in a sling.

"Lady Bethany, you certainly do know how to get into trouble, don't you?" He prattled at me, trying to keep my mind off the pain, I supposed. I listened, but only vaguely, I was too tired.

I could hear the dull explosions of the battle outside. I hoped Erik won. When Aryan was finished with me, I lay back, listening to the sound of war.

The next thing I knew, I was opening my eyes. Erik sat in the chair beside me. He smiled a little.

"Good morning."

"Morning." I sighed. "Did we win?"

He nodded. "Yes, we won."

"Mia? Leo? Eliza?"

"They're all well. Don't worry. You're the only one here."

I grinned. "Good.

"What about Darrell?"

His face fell a bit. "He escaped again. But his army is gone. He can't do any more damage, and we'll catch him soon enough.

"We found the other fairy, too. The one that wanted Daniel to kill you." I nodded. "His name is Lee, and he was a corporal for Darrell. He's in the dungeon now with Marissa."

"Thank goodness. That's one less thing to worry about at night."

"Bethany?"

"Yes?"

"Can I ask you something?"

"Of course."

"How did he get a hold of you?"

I looked at the rug. "My horse knocked us off. A centaur frightened him—"

"Centaur?"

I nodded. "I almost fell off the cliff. Darrell caught me and dragged me back up. I tried to use my powers to get away from him, but they were weak." I looked at him. "I don't understand it."

He watched me with shrewd eyes. "Did you hit your head?"

"No."

"Hmmm...." He thought for a moment. "Well, you're only just starting out; it'll probably take some time for your powers to get stronger."

"You think that's it?"

"Maybe. I've never heard of someone losing their power."

"Must be I'm a freak."

He laughed at me. "No, you're definitely not a freak. Trust me, I know some."

I giggled. Aryan walked in, then. He bowed slightly and moved to check on my arm.

"Think I'll survive?"

"Unfortunately, yes," he teased. He tightened the sling and went back out. I sat up.

"Back here again." I sighed.

"You'll be back in your room by tomorrow," Erik reassured me.

IT TOOK SEVERAL WEEKS for my arm and the cuts on my legs to heal. I couldn't go to the victory ball, but Erik stayed with me that evening, telling me stories about his childhood and his parents. Especially Lady Matilda.

Lady Kat came over the next morning with treats from the ball, and some left-over wine. I thanked her, asked the maids to go find their king wherever he was, and bring him over.

It seemed to me like it was taking a strangely large amount of time for him to get the hole back open. Of course, I wasn't holding out hope, but whenever I asked him he said they were working on it, and it seemed to me that if they were actually working that hard on it, I would be home by now. I wondered more than once whether he was deliberately stalling in order to keep me in the Empire longer.

So even though I was happily situated in the Empire I was even happier when Leo came in to tell me they'd opened the hole back up. I grinned widely.

"Truly?" I bit my lip. I was starting to talk like them.

"Yes, My Lady."

I almost couldn't bear the teary goodbyes of my friends when it was time for me to go. I clung to Mia and Erik most of all and cried, even though I knew he was coming through the hole with me. Only the assurance that this wasn't a final goodbye gave me the guts to go through the Veil.

We stopped, right where our journey had first begun. In the meadow, by the waterfall. Thankfully, not in a tree.

Erik led the way to my car—because I'd forgotten where it was parked—and drove me home. He kissed me forehead when I got out....and then he was gone.

"Bethany! Come on, honey, it's time for dinner."

I jogged up to the porch, back into my mother's arms.

Don't miss out!

Visit the website below and you can sign up to receive emails whenever Ashlyn Pierce publishes a new book. There's no charge and no obligation.

https://books2read.com/r/B-A-OQRO-MYEPB

BOOKS 2 READ

Connecting independent readers to independent writers.

About the Author

Ashlyn Pierce is part fae, part mortal mixed with fairy dust and filled with the magic of a untold thousand stories.

She lives in the rolling hills of Northern New York, where she writes fantasy YA and dystopian novels when she is not skulking through the forest or foraging through her favorite bookstore.

Ashlyn Pierce is the penname of Sarajean Gatch.

Read more at https://www.ashlynpiercenovels.com/.